495

"Not that the story need be long, but it
will take a long while to make it short."
— Henry David Thoreau

Goodbye
Harold,
Good Luck

Audrey Thomas is the author of several novels and story
collections. Born in New York in 1935, she moved to British
Columbia in 1959. She spent two years in Ghana, where her
husband was teaching, and much of her fiction recalls her
life in Africa. She separated from her husband in 1972 and
made her home in an isolated cabin on Galiano Island.

Ms Thomas has taught at many of Canada's universities
and was the recipient of the Scotland-Canada Writer's Award.
Her novel, *Intertidal Life*, was nominated for a Governor
General's Award.

D1016175

GOODBYE HAROLD, GOOD LUCK

Audrey Thomas

Penguin Books

Penguin Books Canada Limited, 2801 John Street, Markham, Ontario,
Canada L3R 1B4
Penguin Books Ltd., Harmondsworth, Middlesex, England
Penguin Books, 40 West 23rd Street, New York, New York 10010 U.S.A.
Penguin Books Australia Ltd., Ringwood, Victoria, Australia
Penguin Books (N.Z.) Ltd., Private Bag, Takapuna, Auckland 9, New Zealand

First published by Penguin Books Canada Limited, 1986

Published in this edition, 1987

Copyright © Audrey Thomas, 1986

All rights reserved.

Manufactured in Canada

Canadian Cataloguing in Publication Data
Thomas, Audrey, 1935–
Goodbye Harold, good luck

(Penguin short fiction)
ISBN 0-14-008809-1

I. Title.   II. Series.

PS8539.H64G66 1987   C813'.54   C86-093414-4
PR9199.3.T45G66 1987

Acknowledgements

"Elevation" first appeared in *Saturday Night*.

"The Man with Clam Eyes" first appeared in *Interface* magazine.

"The Dance" was awarded third prize in the Prism International Fiction Contest and was published in *Prism International*.

"Degrees" was broadcast on CBC's "Anthology" and also published in *Small Wonders*.

"Compulsory Figures" first appeared in the Canadian-Australian journal, *True North/Down Under*.

"Mothering Sunday" first appeared, in a slightly different version, in *Room of One's Own*.

"The Princess and the Zucchini" first appeared in *Prism International*.

To Claire, who doesn't laugh (too hard)
when I look for the iron in the fridge.

Contents

"Adopt the character of the twisting octopus, which takes on the appearance of the nearby rock. Now follow in this direction, now turn a different hue ."

Theognis

Goodbye
Harold,
Good Luck

Introduction

A postcard of an old, wind-up gramophone with a bright red horn. An amaryllis bulb in my shopping bag. I had been to see an exhibit called "The French Connection," French art and artefacts connected with Scotland's history. As I came out into the foyer I couldn't resist a look at the postcard rack. I collect postcards, ostensibly to send but I find them hard to part with and will often buy two of something which takes my fancy — one for me and one for the person I'm thinking of. I have hundreds of postcards in shoeboxes back home.

The amaryllis bulb was for old times' sake, because we usually plant one in a pot in mid-November so that it will burst forth at Christmas-time. We plant red ones, as being brighter, more festive I suppose than white or pink. I have always felt an amaryllis would produce music if only it could, but I thought more in terms of trumpet voluntaries than the thin, scratchy voices that came out from those old cylindrical records, voices that seemed to be the voices of ghosts singing in faint wire-thin tones about love or war or "the green-eyed monster," jealousy. I knew these records. I knew that kind of gramophone. But I had never seen one with a bright red horn, an amaryllis horn. I bought the postcard. I bought two.

We had one of those gramophones, you see. It had been in my father's family for years and had two horns, one rather dull-looking, brass or brass-coloured but not shiny, and the other a "morning-glory horn," as my father called it, of the most beautiful and delicate blue. The records were wax cylinders and each was kept in a padded cardboard cylinder of its own. I thought they were magic (they were). God knows where they (and the gramophone) have got to. I grew up and went away, wanted to find out for myself about love and pain and the green-eyed monster. But there I was now, on a November day in Edinburgh unpacking my shopping bag and smiling as I saw the correspondences between the amaryllis and the gramophone on the postcard and then thinking back to my father letting me wind up an instrument that was an antique even then. And then suddenly remembering a line from one of those far-off mostly forgotten songs: "Who killed her. Who killed the Black Widow?" (If you want to know what those voices sounded like listen to a tape being played back very fast.) Then I thought of how my father used to plant bulbs in bowls for "forcing" into early bloom. And of how he, who loved history, would have loved this city but has long been dead and in the earth himself. "Only connect." And so I began a story.

This is the way my mind works, through correspondences, and this is the way my stories work as well. I move into thought only through my senses, particularly my visual sense although the others as well. My oldest daughter said to me once that she couldn't stand the smell of Dettol, which was the antiseptic they had used in Ghana and she had been ill, quite ill, while we were there in the sixties. I told her I had mixed feelings about it. I too had been ill, weeks in hospital while we were out there, and Dettol brings back all the terror and sadness of that experience. But Dettol was also used in the hospital in England where she was born and that reminds me of a very happy time, the feel of my first baby in my arms and the wonder that I had had anything to do with creating someone so perfect.

Here, it is the sudden smell of coal smoke as I walk through the city and remember being a student at St Andrews thirty years ago. The senses are my stepping-stones across the floods of experience, how to get from one side to the other (and back again). In a story, of course, I am in control — or I hope I am — and I can lay down, for the reader, the particular stones I want her or him to use. Thus it is very important, in the story called "Miss Foote" that the phrase is "That man is following me everywhere." It is important, in terms of her CND affiliations, that the walking stick she carries, her father's walking stick which he needed after spending years in a prisoner-of-war camp, is carved with "dragons ready to breathe fire." The rhyme, "Round and round the garden" is important, the phrase, "diminished responsibility." All these have been placed there by me the writer to help you the reader towards a — towards a what? James Joyce, being Catholic born and bred, called it an epiphany. I, Protestant Irish that I am, am not sure that's exactly the word I want. How about, thinking back to my amaryllis, which is just poking its green fingernail through the earth, "a new blooming."

I tend to think of myself as a novelist, but I have written many more short stories than I have novels, and I must admit that people seem to like my stories better than my novels. Last year I realized with some amazement that I have been publishing stories for twenty years. I am, obviously, fascinated by a different kind of tension here than what I find in the novel, although I often write a story and later — even years later — say to myself, "hmmm, I'm not finished with that, let's open it up a bit more." My novel *Mrs. Blood* began life as a short story as did *Latakia*, as did *Intertidal Life*. (And "Elevation," from this collection, is now an hour-long radio drama, another form I love to work in.)

Some people say I am not political enough, not feminist enough in my writing. I'm never quite sure what they mean. Recently I heard the South African writer André Brink speak at Edinburgh University. He said, "The writer who writes to promote a cause would do better to embrace politics openly." I believe this wholeheartedly. You can't add "feminism" to a story the way you can add vanilla to a cake, sticking your finger in and tasting, "needs a bit more vanilla" (or lemon or almond essence). I consider myself a feminist but I do not, consciously, think about feminism when I am making a story. And I am interested in points of view, even points of view I see as immature, silly or unenlightened. I remember a character in *Songs My Mother Taught Me*. She is one of the grandfather's succession of slightly bizarre housekeepers and she gives the little girl, Isobel, her first taste of beer.

"Ugh," says Isobel. "It tastes terrible."

"Honey," replies the housekeeper, "it tastes terrible — to you."

Audrey Thomas
Edinburgh, 1986

Elevation

Elevation

She met him first in August at an ice-cream social given by her friend Robert. She did not pay too much attention to him then, or no more than she was paying to the other guests — which is to say quite a lot, being who she was, a listener, an observer; but she didn't single him out for special attention. That would come later. In August she had only recently returned from hospital and was still feeling a bit strange, things alternately too fuzzy or almost unbearably clear, so she had been given a *chaise-longue* on the veranda and a glass of punch and was told to relax and enjoy herself.

There were three ice-cream-makers in action, everyone taking turns with cranking, including her daughter, who had never done this before. She was half asleep from the sunshine and punch and murmur of voices when she heard someone say, "Ah, here comes the man now; here comes the Emperor of Ice Cream himself, here's the expert." After some talk and laughter inside the house, where Robert's daughter was strumming a guitar and a group of her friends were softly singing, a smiling man with a round, benevolent face — the kind of face she used to imagine she saw on the man in the moon — came out onto the veranda carrying a large covered basket. With a magician's flourish he pulled out Mason jars full of fruits and nuts and jewelled syrups, holding each one up to the light before placing it on the round table by the door. He said that the ferry had been late, and he and Robert embraced warmly. Nobody introduced him but he seemed to know most of the crowd already. (The next day she found out from Robert that one of the women there was his ex-wife, his second ex-wife to be exact, but she didn't remember the woman at all.)

She watched him through half-closed eyes, watched him being warm and friendly, never staying in one place very long, sitting down and then jumping up to take a turn with the ice-cream or volunteering to go up to the fish camp for more ice. At one point he spoke to her daughter, who was filling two bowls with blackberry ice-cream. "Save room for some of my fresh peach," he said to her, smiling. His voice, if not exactly southern, was certainly country. Her daughter explained that one bowl was for her mother and he looked around to see which woman that was. "Over there," her daughter said, "on the *chaise*." He smiled again but didn't hurry over, only came and sat down just as she was thinking she'd had enough and better be getting home. He spoke to her briefly in that soft country accent and told her what a pretty daughter she had.

She thought to herself that it would be perfect if his name were Floyd or Earle and he ran a gas station somewhere in Oregon or Montana; but since he was one of Robert's friends it wouldn't be that simple.

Robert's friends all seemed to live lives of carefully orchestrated poverty, although she felt that there was money behind them, perhaps trust funds from dead grandmothers, something like that. And education too. If you asked the right questions, it usually turned out that they'd been to Berkeley or Yale or Columbia. You wouldn't know it to look at them, of course; that was part of the game. They were weavers, makers of stained glass, painters or writers or musicians. That is, when asked, what they said they did; but they had done something else first, and for a long time, something which, if it were talked about at all, was shrugged off with a laugh, part of a past they were quite willing to forget. Robert sold wood-stoves and wore a T-shirt that said "Split wood, not atoms" on the back. He had jars of different flours and dried fruits on shelves in the entrance way. One was labelled NFM in his neat handwriting. When people asked, he said "Not for Munchies. Those are special, just for me." They were peyote buttons.

He also kept a few rust-coloured hens, who ranged freely in the yard during the daytime. Lately he had taken up EST.

("Humming-birds," Robert says to her on the phone the next day, when she calls to thank him for the party. "His name is Clayton and he studies humming-birds." "As a hobby?" she asks, thinking that would fit right in with Robert and his friends. Some ex-engineer with a private income who was now "into" humming-birds. Robert laughs, "Hardly. He's a zoologist. He's obsessed by them." "How interesting," she says. So is he one of you or not, she wants to say.)

She and Robert have not been close friends for very long, although she had heard his name often enough and seen him at the Friday market or on the ferries. Two summers earlier she had even spent an afternoon at the beach with a group of women and children, including Robert's wife (now ex-) and her daughter. Robert interested her, not romantically, but as an example of something. The American Boy-Man, perhaps — the Eternal Boy. It was something to do with his smile and a certain innocence. There had been several of these boy-men at the ice-cream social: charming, interesting to sit next to. But perhaps scary to spend your life with. Most of them were Americans, as Robert was, as she had been once, technically, but had never really felt herself to be. Lying in bed the night of the ice-cream social, she had thought to herself, "They're all so American," then wondered what on earth she had meant by that. And she realized that she hadn't been in love with an American since she was nineteen years old.

(That one had dropped her after a steamy evening in a car in Cambridge, Massachusetts, when he had whispered, "Oh God, I want to make love to you," and she had given the wrong answer, she had answered, "I think that would be lovely." Whereupon he had sat up and turned on the ignition and taken her straight back to her hotel. Nice girls didn't say things like that. He never really forgave her and they soon broke up.)

The Americans she had met here on the island and in Canada generally were charming, for the most part. They led admirable and enviable lives — kept goats or chickens, cooked on woodstoves (Robert was a superb cook, as was — she was to discover later — Clayton). They joined Amnesty International and supported Greenpeace; they often lived in hand-built houses and almost always had fruit trees and vegetable gardens.

They had friendly rivalries to see who had the first peas up. Yet for some vague reason which, she admitted, might lie within herself, they made her uneasy. Robert's house was beautiful and orderly. He baked his own bread (even ground his own flour), planted Iceland poppies in among the rocks. And yet. And yet.

(One thing about Clayton — he made this clear early on — he didn't come from any well-to-do family like Robert's or some of those others. His father had been a railwayman and proud of it. Nothin' fancy about him, no sir! Just his fancy brain.)

The following winter, during the rather dreary months, when it was too wet to do more than look at seed catalogues and there wasn't much going on socially, she and Robert and some of their other friends decided to hold pot-luck suppers every other Saturday. This turned out to be a lot of fun, and in March she dreamed up the idea of a welcome-to-springtime party to which everyone would have to bring something green. Robert had a new girlfriend as well as a winter beard, so he said he was going to dye it green and have Suzanne shave it off at the party. "Sounds a little too much like Samson and Delilah to me," she said, "but do it, do it. We can all sit around and watch." Then she suggested he invite his friend Clayton to come over. "He can bring some pistachio ice-cream."

That night was the beginning of their friendship — if that's what it was. At one point Clayton, who was quite stoned when he arrived and spent a long time going from room to room in her small house, picking up objects, looking at what she had put up on the walls, told a story about his daughter, who lived with her mother somewhere in the States. She had been accidentally left in a coffin when her class was having a workshop on dying and death. She heard the class leave, and then the teacher, and then there she was, all alone. He told how she didn't panic, knowing the teacher would remember and come back, just kept saying to herself, "Now then Em'ly, now then Em'ly," and taking deep breaths the way he'd taught her to do when she was in a tight situation and feelin kinda scared. The teacher was surprised, when she rushed back in a panic, to find Emily sound asleep.

She looked at her own daughter, who was a little younger than the Emily in the story. "Bullshit," she mouthed, and her daughter grinned. (But still they both admired his dark and curly hair.)

Now it is May and he is over on the island to catch some humming-birds for his research project. She has seen him several times since March and they have exchanged telephone calls and letters. She knows that he has neat black notebooks going back years — each year is clearly labelled on the spine. They contain memories, dreams, reflections, thoughts on perception, on language, on decision-making. There are maps and drawings and the occasional letter from an old girlfriend. The notebooks are not personal, although they contain some intensely personal details. She realizes with a shock that he expects to be famous. They are something he is sure will be read and admired by strangers at some point in the future. He talks about rates of accomplishment and degrees of involvement, discusses optimal foraging, nectar availability, genetic longevity. She copies down some phrases that appeal to her, such as this remark by William Bateson: "The brain can receive only news of difference."

She begins to realize that if he is studying humming-birds, she is studying him. She is fascinated by people with obsessions, having one or two of her own. In one place he writes, "There is a whole world let loose in my head right now," and she smiles at his excitement.

The first time she really talks to him about his work, she asks him how much a humming-bird weighs. He forages in his pockets, then shakes his head and says, "Well, I guess this will have to do." He holds out her hand, palm up, and places a dime on it. She notices that it is an old Franklin D. Roosevelt dime. "Imagine that there are two of these," he says. Later Robert tells her that Clayton often does this — rummages in his pocket but can only come up with one dime instead of two. So what she feels that day is half the weight of a humming-bird.

His hands flutter when he talks — they soar and dip. He says things like, "Let's see if this idea gets off the ground." His big interest is decision-making — that's what he needs the birds for, that's why he is over here today with his two graduate students. Dinner will be early, so that they will be free to deal with the birds at dusk.

The feeders they have brought along are nasty plastic things with red plastic flowers arranged around nectar holes. The flowers look like strange, brightly lipsticked mouths. She is surprised that the birds are taken in, but it's the nectar they're after — their interest is not aesthetic. She imagines drinking from one of those things as the equivalent of eating a good picnic lunch off paper plates. And many people have feeders over here, some of them of equal ugliness. It amuses her when he says that you must never feed humming-birds honey; they get a disease like thrush, and the throat closes over. She wonders how many humming-birds died over here in the sixties, when nobody would've been caught dead using sugar.

She asks about the colour red. It seems to be important to vertebrates, he says. A male robin will go absolutely crazy at a large patch of red. He "sees" it as the breast of an enormous robin. She thinks of those heavily lipsticked mouths. She thinks of the red satin dresses of Hollywood sirens. She thinks of how when she was young she and her friends played a game where you counted a hundred red convertibles and then the next man you saw was the man you were going to marry.

The birds will be taken to the city and then out to the university, where they will participate in a study on decision-making. He has always before studied humming-birds in high meadows; he does not like the idea of capturing them, but it's necessary. "Consistent choice," he writes in his journal, "implies the ability to discriminate between alternatives and also suggests preference for some alternatives over others." The longer she knows him, the more she tries to come to some decisions of her own.

"Do you ever see them hesitate?" she asks.

"The birds? Why of course."

He has given her some of his papers to read. She finds it heavy going. There are many words she simply does not understand. She keeps a piece of paper by her right hand as she reads, just as she does when she's reading a book or a newspaper in French, and writes down all the words she doesn't know. And in her notebook she writes down things about him, the story of the dime, the way his hands flutter and fly, the way he started telling her about what keeps an airplane up and then suddenly said, "When I was flying to X to get my vasectomy undone…"

One day she comes across a phrase she particularly likes. "On the immediate level of events occurring in meadows." She is not sure what it means but she likes the sound of it. "On the immediate level of events occurring in meadows."

He loves Vancouver for its sidewalks and umbrellas. There were no sidewalks in the small town he came from and a real man would never carry an umbrella. They built the highway to Panama City right past his front door. He and his friends used to go up on a hill with handfuls of rocks and throw them at the earth-moving machines, pretending they were grenades, blowing up the whole damn works. Trucks rolled past the house all night.

"What is 'sessile'?" she asks.

"Rooted to one point," he says, "like a tree. Fastened down. Occupying a single point on a plane. We also occupy points on a plane, but the points we occupy can be different at different times. However, unless we use machines, the points are continuous; they exist on the same plane. That plane represents our freedom."

"We live in two dimensions," he says, "not like a fish or a bird. It's volume that makes the difference."

She reads him John Donne's poem where the soul of the beloved is the fixed foot of the compass around which the lover moves. And then, embarrassed, she closes the book and says, "I don't really like them, you know — humming-birds. They seem more like insects than birds. And they dive at you. And at each other. They seem very aggressive."

"Oh they are, they are," he cries, "they have to be!

But what I'm seeing with the humming-birds is that they pack themselves into the available resource space and take whatever advantage they can."

"Sounds just like man," she says, and he smiles. His face really does "light up" when he smiles, she thinks. He really is the man in the moon.

"Rufous humming-birds," she writes in her notebook. "Calliope."

He won't sit still. He moves around her kitchen, checking it out, seeing what spices she has, whether she uses "real" coffee. Talking all the time. "In some language or other," he says, "the word for 'eat' changes depending on whether you are standing or sitting, indoors or out, et cetera. And some primitive languages are predominantly verbs."

"Well, *sit down* then," she wants to say, "and *shut up.*" When he gets really wound up, his small-town accent becomes more and more pronounced, as if saying to her, to the world, "I'm not really an intellectual, I'm still just a boy from Chico, California."

"This coffee's real good," he says.

Gradually his childhood takes shape for her, takes on flesh. She thinks she likes his mother best so far. His mother had a Whammo slingshot she kept on a nail by the kitchen door. And a little pile of pebbles on the windowsill. Whenever a dog came into her vegetable garden, she'd grab the slingshot and let fly. She was a terrific shot and could get the dog in the left hind leg every time. He had a slingshot, too, and went robin hunting. He'd line up the dead robins in the ditch between the back alley and the garden. Just study them, see how they were put together. Later, when he was a bit older, he had a .22 rifle and loaded it with a hollow-point .22 shell. He shot a bird, a stellar jay, as it flew directly above him. "It rained guts and blood and bones all over me and something went click right then. Something about killing for the hell of it or even just for study. I have a hard time with that one, I surely do."

His mother goes to his father's grave, puts flowers on it and just stands there. He wonders what she is thinking, what remembering. He smiles. She can see that he's fond of his mother.

She decides to be motherly herself and make gingerbread with whipped cream. Her whole house smells of spices. Her daughter is staying overnight with friends, so at five o'clock she puts the cake in her basket, together with a bottle of wine, and walks the short distance to where he and his two students are staying. They are fixing the nets to long, thin poles. The nets are black and very fine, and for just a few minutes, at dusk, they will become invisible. They are like the nets her mother used to put over the black-currant bushes. (But those were to keep the birds away.)

He is very excited and gives her a hug. He is pleased to see that she has brought her notebook. "I've brought gingerbread and whipped cream and wine as well," she says.

"Good girl."

After all the nets and feeders are in place, up here above the sea and down below, across the road in the meadow, they sit down to eat. The stew is delicious, but the air is full of tension. He can hardly wait to get started. At dusk the three men hurry out, but she decides to sit a while by the Franklin stove.

Soon he is back, running, grabbing her hand, insisting she come and watch; so they run down the path in the gathering darkness, then stand, hand in hand in the meadow, hardly breathing, waiting. Soon she hears the strange buzzing whine but cannot see the bird.

"There's one," he whispers, then drops her hand, moves forward quickly to pluck it off the net.

He comes back to her, his hands together, cupped gently around the bird, holding it out to her as though he is about to offer her a drink of water. His hands are shaking. Or is the bird doing it to him, frantic — is it really the bird's heart beating?

"Do you want to hold it?" he whispers. "Hold out your hands."

She puts her hands behind her back. "No. I don't want to."

Still holding the humming-bird he leans over and kisses her.

"I don't like it either," he whispers. "I don't like this part of it at all."

The Man With
Clam Eyes

The Man With Clam Eyes

I came to the sea because my heart was broken. I rented a cabin from an old professor who stammered when he talked. He wanted to go far away and look at something. In the cabin there is a table, a chair, a bed, a woodstove, an aladdin lamp. Outside there is a well, a privy, rocks, trees and the sea.

(The lapping of waves, the scream of gulls.)

I came to this house because my heart was broken. I brought wine in green bottles and meaty soup bones. I set an iron pot on the back of the stove to simmer. I lit the lamp. It was no longer summer and the wind grieved around the door. Spiders and mice disapproved of my arrival. I could hear them clucking their tongues in corners.

(The sound of the waves and the wind.)

This house is spotless, shipshape. Except for the spiders. Except for the mice in corners, behind the walls. There are no clues. I have brought with me wine in green bottles, an eiderdown quilt, my brand-new *Bartlett's Familiar Quotations.* On the inside of the front jacket it says, "Who said: 1. In wildness is the preservation of the world. 2. All hell broke loose. 3. You are the sunshine of my life."

I want to add another. I want to add two more. Who said, "There is no nice way of saying this?" Who said, "Let's not go over it again?"   The wind grieves around the door. I stuff the cracks with rags torn from the bottom of my skirt. I am sad. Shall I leave here then? Shall I go and lie outside his door calling whoo — whoo — whoo like the wind?

(The sound of the waves and the wind.)

I drink all of the wine in one green bottle. I am like a glove. Not so much shapeless as empty, waiting to be filled up. I set my lamp in the window, I sleep to the sound of the wind's grieving.

(Quiet breathing, the wind still there, but soft, then gradually fading out. The passage of time, then seagulls, and then waves.)

How can I have slept when my heart is broken? I dreamt of a banquet table under green trees. I was a child and ate ripe figs with my fingers. Now I open the door —

(West-coast birds, the towhee with its strange cry, and the waves.)

The sea below is rumpled and wrinkled and the sun is shining. I can see islands and then more islands, as though my island had spawned islands in the night. The sun is shining. I have never felt so lonely in my life. I go back in. I want to write a message and throw it out to sea. I rinse my wine bottle from last night and set it above the stove to dry. I sit at the small table thinking. My message must be clear and yet compelling, like a lamp lit in a window on a dark night. There is a blue bowl on the table and a rough spoon carved from some sweet-smelling wood. I eat porridge with raisins while I think. The soup simmers on the back of the stove. The seagulls outside are riding the wind and crying ME ME ME. If this were a fairy tale, there would be someone here to help me, give me a ring, a cloak, a magic word. I bang on the table in my frustration. A small drawer pops open.

(Sound of the wind the waves lapping.)

Portents and signs mean something, point to something, otherwise — too cruel. The only thing in the drawer is part of a manuscript, perhaps some secret hobby of the far-off professor. It is a story about a man on a train from Genoa to Rome. He has a gun in his pocket and is going to Rome to kill his wife. After the conductor comes through, he goes along to the lavatory, locks the door, takes out the gun, then stares at himself in the mirror. He is pleased to note that his eyes are clear and clam. *Clam?* Pleased to note that his eyes are clear and clam? I am not quick this morning. It takes me a while before I see what has happened. And then I laugh. How can I laugh when my heart is cracked like a dropped plate? But I laugh at the man on the train to Rome, staring at himself in the mirror — the man with clam eyes. I push aside the porridge and open my *Bartlett's Familiar Quotations*. I imagine Matthew Arnold — "The sea is clam tonight…" or Wordsworth — "It is a beauteous evening, clam and free…" I know what to say in my message.

The bottle is dry. I take the piece of paper and push it in. Then the cork, which I seal with wax from a yellow candle. I will wait just before dark.

(The waves, the lapping sea. The gulls, loud and then gradually fading out. Time passes.)

Men came by in a boat with a pirate flag. They were diving for sea urchins and when they saw me sitting on the rocks they gave me one. They tell me to crack it open and eat the inside, here, they will show me how. I cry No and No, I want to watch it for a while. They shrug and swim away.   All afternoon I watched it in pleasant idleness. I had corrected the typo of course — I am that sort of person — but the image of the man with clam eyes wouldn't leave me and I went down on the rocks to think. That's when I saw the divers with their pirate flag; that's when I was given the gift of the beautiful maroon sea urchin. The rocks were as grey and wrinkled as elephants, but warm, with enormous pores and pools licked out by the wind and the sea. The sea urchin is a dark maroon, like the lips of certain black men I have known. It moves constantly back/forth, back/forth with all its spines turning. I take it up to the cabin. I let it skate slowly back and forth across the table. I keep it wet with water from my bucket. The soup smells good. This morning I add carrots, onions, potatoes, bay leaves and thyme. How can

I be hungry when my heart is broken? I cut bread with a long, sharp knife, holding the loaf against my breast. Before supper I put the urchin back into the sea.

(Sound of the wind and the waves.)

My bottle is ready and there is a moon. I have eaten soup and drunk wine and nibbled at my bread. I have read a lot of un-familiar quotations. I have trimmed the wick and lit the lamp and set it in the window. The sea is still tonight and the moon has left a long trail of silver stretching almost to the rocks.

(Night sounds. A screech owl. No wind, but
the waves lapping.)

I go down to the sea as far as I can go. I hold the corked bottle in my right hand and fling it towards the stars. For a moment I think that a hand has reached up and caught it as it fell back towards the sea. I stand there. The moon and the stars light up my loneliness. How will I fall asleep when my heart is broken?

(Waves, then fading out. The sound of the
wild birds calling.)

I awoke with the first bird. I lay under my eiderdown and watched my breath in the cold room. I wondered if the birds could understand one another, if a chickadee could talk with a junco, for example. I wondered whether, given the change in seasons and birds, there was always the same first bird. I got up and lit the fire and put a kettle on for washing.

(The iron stove is opened and wood lit.
It catches, snaps and crackles.
Water is poured into a large kettle.)

When I went outside to fling away the water, he was
there, down on the rocks below me, half-man, half-fish.
His green scales glittered like sequins in the winter
sunlight. He raised his arm and beckoned to me.

(Sound of the distant gulls.)

We have been swimming. The water is cold, cold,
cold. Now I sit on the rocks, combing out my hair. He
tells me stories. My heart darts here and there like a
frightened fish. The tracks of his fingers run silver
along my leg. He told me that he is a drowned sailor,
that he went overboard in a storm at sea. He speaks
with a strong Spanish accent.

He has been with the traders who bought for a pit-
tance the sea-otters' pelts which trimmed the robes of
Chinese mandarins. A dozen glass beads would be
bartered with the Indians for six of the finest skins.

With Cook he observed the transit of Venus
in the cloudless skies of Tahiti.

With Drake he had sailed on "The Golden
Hind" for the Pacific Coast. They landed in a bay off
California. His fingers leave silver tracks on my bare
legs. I like to hear him say it — Cal-ee fórn-ya. The Indians there were friendly. The men were naked but the
women wore petticoats of bulrushes.

Oh how I like it when he does that.

He was blown around the Cape of Good Hope with
Diaz. Only they called it the Cape of Storms. The King
did not like the name and altered it.   Oh.

His cool tongue laps me. My breasts bloom in the moonlight. We dive — and rise out of the sea, gleaming. He decorates my hair with clamshells and stars, my body with sea-lettuce. I do not feel the cold. I laugh. He gives me a rope of giant kelp and I skip for him in the moonlight. He breaks open the shells of mussels and pulls out their sweet flesh with his long fingers. We tip the liquid into our throats; it tastes like tears.   He touches me with his explorer's hands.

(Waves, the sea — loud — louder. Fading out.)

I ask him to come with me, up to the professor's cabin. "It is impóss-ee-ble," he says. He asks me to go with him. "It is impóss-ee-ble," I say. "Not at all."
I cannot breathe in the water. I will drown. I have no helpful sisters. I do not know a witch.

(Sea, waves, grow louder, fade,
fading but not gone.)

He lifts me like a wave and carries me towards the water. I can feel the roll of the world. My legs dissolve at his touch and flow together. He shines like a green fish in the moonlight. "Is easy," he says, as my mouth fills up with tears. "Is nothing." The last portions of myself begin to shift and change.
I dive beneath the waves! He clasps me to him. We are going to swim to the edges of the world, he says, and I believe him.
I take one glance backwards and wave to the woman in the window. She has lit the lamp. She is eating soup and drinking wine. Her heart is broken. She is thinking about a man on a train who is going to kill his wife. The lamp lights up her loneliness. I wish her well.

Miss Foote

Miss Foote

The night was dark and stormy
The rain came down in torrents.
The King said unto Antonio,
"Antonio tell us a tale."
Antonio began as follows:
"The night was dark and stormy
The rain came down in torrents.
The King said unto Antonio,
'Antonio, tell us a tale.'
Antonio began as follows...."

Miss Foote liked to think of herself as a traveller, not a tourist. And she enjoyed travelling alone. No one to consult or complain if she wanted to pop down past one more narrow passage in the bazaar or get up at dawn to see the sun rise over the Ganges. There was nothing she liked better, she said, then being in a strange city, with a map and having to sort things out for herself. If the map were in some foreign language, so much the better. Miss Foote could say "where is?" "how much?" "too much," "please" and "thank you" in eleven languages, including Urdu. She had also learned "That man is following me everywhere" but had never, so far, had need of it. Once, on Philoppapou Hill in Athens, a man in a ragged overcoat had stepped from behind a bush and exposed himself. "Put that disgusting thing away!" cried Miss Foote, raising her walking stick, and the man fled. The walking stick had belonged to Daddy, who had been a missionary in China. It was elaborately carved with dragons, mouths open, ready to breathe fire. Miss Foote and her brother Edward had been born in Singapore, twins, just after Daddy had been put in a prisoner-of-war camp by the Japanese. He was a scholar by nature and had completed an English-Chinese dictionary while he was in prison. He came out limping and weighing only seven stone, but he said that those years were a godsend in a way because there was nothing for him to do and he had the time to write. He was a member of the Plymouth Brethren, and if you didn't know who *they* were, Miss Foote was happy to tell you. She had a tendency to stand, or lean, too close to you as she talked, so that after a while you had the feeling that the two of you were trapped together in a lift, or something even smaller, a public telephone box perhaps. But you couldn't help liking her just the same — she had a kind of innocence that was marvellous to see in a woman her age. If you came down to breakfast at the Bed and Breakfast or Pension or Small Hotel where you and Miss Foote both happened to be staying, she would look out at the rain or the grey skies and call, "Clearing by noon! It's right here in the papers."

And if, at the end of your holiday, in a moment of

magnanimity, after Miss Foote had brought out her
address book and written her address on a card, "Miss
Agnes Foote, 14 Small Oaks Road, Edgbaston, Birmingham," if in such a moment you happened to say
"Well, Miss Foote, if you are ever in Boston (or Toronto or Sydney or Aberdeen) do look us up — can't com-
pare with the Trans-Siberian Railway, of course, or sailing down the Nile — " chances were you would get a
jolly letter a few months later saying that it so happened she *would* be passing through Toronto (or Aberdeen or Sydney or Boston) and could she possibly stop
for a few days. She was always very careful about it and
gave you plenty of warning, not like some people who
send a postcard which arrives after they do or who,
worse yet, ring you up from the station. No, Miss Foote
was all right (if only she didn't stand so close to you
when she told all her amusing stories). She would take
the dogs for walks and spend hours down on the floor
playing games with the kiddies (who sometimes made
fun of her behind her back). Miss Foote liked children,
although alas she had none of her own. Before her
retirement she had been Deputy Head of an Infant and
Junior School. She loved the Prayers every morning
when all the children would assemble and show their
hankies (the school was not in a very nice district; in
fact you might call it a slum) and call out "Good Morning Miss Goodall," "Good Morning Miss Foote" and so
on down the line of teachers; and then Miss Foote, who
played the piano a little bit, would thump out "All
Things Bright and Beautiful."

Some of the older children were not so nice,
especially the boys, but she taught Class Three, the six-
and seven-year-olds. Carefully she printed on the
blackboard:

THE NORTH WIND DOTH BLOW
AND WE SHALL HAVE SNOW
AND WHAT WILL THE ROBIN DO THEN
POOR THING?

and walked up and down the rows as the children bent their heads and bit their lips and tried to copy her writing. It was thanks to Miss Foote that twenty years ago bathtubs had been installed in one of the school's outbuildings. There was no need for children to be dirty, at least not children in her care. As she scrubbed the dirty little necks and washed and combed the tangled heads of hair (checking for nits and dealing promptly with any cases of same) she thought wistfully of the children she might have had if anyone had asked her to marry. Nowadays it was so much easier — in that regard at least. If a young woman wanted to be a mother, it was quite all right for her not to have a husband. If she couldn't find anyone suitable, she could always adopt.

Miss Foote's ideas were really very up to date. She had participated in more than one protest march and she also believed in abortion on demand. She was convinced that if a mother didn't want the child, right from the beginning, the child knew it — it influenced his personality. Most criminals, Miss Foote would declare, were undoubtedly unwanted children.

Miss Foote is now in Cornwall for a fortnight. She has been having some slight problem with her heart and the doctor has suggested mild exercise and a few days by the sea. Miss Foote has never been ill a day in her adult life, not really, and she is not only outraged at this mutiny on the part of her heart, she is also a little bit frightened. After the war her family settled in

Australia and she was the only one, later on, who decided to come HOME. She writes to Edward and his family once a year, at Christmas, and sends a few sweets and books for the children, but she has no relatives here in England. She goes to visit the school where she taught but there is a new headmistress now and Miss Foote knows she is not really welcome, that she is "in the way." She has spent most of her free time (and since her retirement all of her time has been free time) travelling. She has hundreds of acquaintances but no friends, not even a dog or a cat or a budgie; a pet would tie her down. She had been planning a trip to Vancouver, flying to Montreal and then crossing Canada by train, ending up with a week's visit to some friends in Victoria, B.C. She called them "friends" when talking to the doctor, but really they were just a nice Canadian family she had known for ten days on a Greek Island ("If you are ever in Victoria," they said) and she had kept in touch. Now perhaps she would never see the Rocky Mountains or take a ferry from Vancouver across to Vancouver Island. (So confusing, all these Vancouvers, until you looked at the map.) She was very angry at her heart for playing up this way.

"You will have to tell your friends," said the doctor, not unkindly, "that you must put off your journey for a while." He gave her some nitroglycerine tablets, in case of pain, and advised her to stop whatever she was doing before she got exhausted.

"I'm a great walker!" Miss Foote cried. "I can't imagine not being able to tramp about just as I please!"

"*Mild* exercise," said the doctor. He had a small, pokey waiting-room and sometimes one had to wait for hours, but Miss Foote never minded; she talked to the mothers or played with the children.

Round and Round the Garden
Like a Teddy Bear —
One Step
Two Step —

She often let a mother with a sick child go ahead of her. "I've got all the time in the world," she always said. All the time in the world. And now here was the doctor telling her that time might be running out. Well, she wouldn't give in. She went home and immediately sat down and thought about where she would go. There was a small fishing village in Cornwall she had been to some years ago. Wonderful walks along the cliffs. She had walked all the way from Port Isaac to Tintagel, seven-and-a-half hours of arduous walking, scrambling in some places. The man in the newsagents, who had sold her the footpath map, looked at her chunky body, her grey hair and warned her that that part of the footpath was for Experienced Hikers only. She smiled sweetly and told him about mountain-climbing in Kashmir (well, it really was a mountain even if they were taken most of the way up in a Land Rover). She showed him Daddy's walking stick — "it's never let me down yet!" She leaned over the counter where all the newspapers were displayed and tapped him on the chest.

"And *you*, young man, you look as though you could do with some sunshine and fresh air."

But there were other, less strenuous walks around Port Isaac, and the place wouldn't be crowded so early in the season. She called the small hotel where she had stayed before and then began to pack. She saw her heart as a naughty child who needed to be taught a lesson. "Firmness," she said to herself, "moderation yes but firmness above all." She wrapped her walking shoes in a plastic carrier bag, tucked them in the corner of her suitcase and strapped the walking stick to the outside. Already she felt better. She locked the door and left a note for the milkman.

"Val de ri," she sang as she walked down the street to the bus-stop. "Val de ra, Val de ri, Val de ra-ha-ha-ha-ha-ha." Two teenagers, with spiked hair coloured like exotic parrots, stopped to look at her as she passed. They did look silly but of course it was all to do with the threat of nuclear war. There would be no prisoners taken in that one, no gentle scholars working on dictionaries. She smiled at them and pointed to the WOMEN FOR PEACE button on her lapel.

"Silly old git," the boy said under his breath but Miss Foote didn't hear him. Val de ri, Val de ra, she was already tramping along the Cornish coast path.

Miss Foote is having a dream. It is Sunday morning and she has started up the path which will lead on to the cliffs. It is about 9:45 and the recorded church bells are ringing. Miss Foote finds it very strange that the church uses a tape of church bells and not a very good tape at that. They have a ridiculous, mechanical sound. Better no church bells at all than that silly racket. Then, as she stops to rest a minute and take a picture of the little fishing boats in the harbour down below (the tide is out and they are lying almost on their sides), the bells stop and a recorded hymn begins.

Christ the Lord is Risen To-day-ay
Ah-ah-ah-ah-al-lay-lew-oo-ya
Sons of Men and Angels Say-ay

Miss Foote is puzzled. It is not Easter Sunday — what an

extraordinary hymn to have chosen. Oh well, it is somewhat better than those awful bells.

As she nears the top of the hill, she sees a young man, dressed all in black except for his white plimsolls, standing right in the middle of the path, reading a newspaper. She is finding the climb a bit difficult and doesn't want to stop until she is at the top. "Coming through!" she calls cheerily to the young man but he doesn't move. "Coming through!" she calls again. Is he deaf? Can he be that absorbed in what he is reading? She will have to go around him, to step off onto the grass; but really, how annoying! She moves to the left and without looking up he does the same. "I want to get by," Miss Foote says. She is breathless from the climb and her heart is pounding heavily. Perhaps the boy is simple. Or maybe he is on drugs. But at ten o'clock on a Sunday morning? She moves back on to the path but he is too quick for her.

"Please let me by," she says, trying not to be afraid.

"Headless Corpse Kept in Sauna Five Months," he says, without looking up. "Nice," he says in disgust. "Oh very very nice."

Miss Foote concludes that he is not quite all there and perhaps a bit deaf to boot. She raises her voice and takes a step forward. She speaks slowly, loudly and distinctly.

"Please — let — me — pass."

The boy lowers the newspaper and stares at her as though he has just become aware of her presence. He has painted his face white, as some of them do these days, and a small part of Miss Foote's mind, a part that has not yet given way to a sense of panic, thinks that he matches up, in his black suit, white face and white shoes, with the black-and-white cows munching con-

tentedly on the hill beyond. Except that they are fat —
this boy is as thin as a rake.

The boy stares at her for a long time; Miss Foote
stares back.

"No," he says finally. "The pathway's closed."
"What do you mean, *closed*?" cries Miss Foote, gen-
uinely indignant. "This is a *public* footpath; it is always
open. I have come up here for a walk and I intend to
have one. Now please get out of my way."

"No," he says and picks up his newspaper again.

Miss Foote looks behind. Surely there must be someone coming, a couple, or a single hiker walking the
coast path early, before it gets too warm.

No one. She sees no one.

The young man lowers his paper again and addresses
her.

"Terrible, don't you think, the way the world is. Nasty,
that's it. It's a nasty world. What chance has anybody
got? A bloke like me, for instance?"

"Young man," says Miss Foote, having recovered her
courage with her breath, "I am not prepared to discuss
the state of the world with you. I wish only to get on
with my walk."

She steps to the left. He steps to the left. She steps
back on the path. He is there before her. To the right it
is a long way down to the sea. Seagulls wheel and
wrangle. It makes her dizzy to think of that long way
down.

"Not much fun knowing what's happening to you, is
it?" he says. "Sometimes don't you wish you was a
Mongol?" He takes a step forward and they are almost
touching.

Miss Foote takes a step back. She is angry and afraid.
If he won't let her by, then he won't. She will go back

down, her Sunday morning ruined, and report him to the police.

"Well, young man," she says in her most severe voice, "I don't know what your game is, but I for one am not amused. And I shall report you to the authorities at my earliest opportunity."

She turns around to start back down the path but he blocks her way.

"No," he says.

"What do you mean no!" (her heart thudding, thudding, like boots banging against her chest, she — must — not — get — up — set). "Now let me pass, let me go back. I've given up trying to go on — surely you're satisfied with that?"

"No," he says, quietly. She can see the spots on his skin underneath the white greasepaint.

Suddenly she is enraged. Never mind her heart, never mind not getting upset, she will not tolerate this insolence. She raises her father's cane and brings it down on the boy's head again and again and again, all the time screaming at him — No, is it? No, is it? I'll give you NO! And then a loud knocking. Her heart? No. What then?

"Miss Foote, Miss Foote, are you all right?" It was the landlady's voice.

Oh God, she is not on the cliff. She is in bed, in the Green Acres Hotel, her right hand still clenched as though holding tight to her walking stick.

The landlady's voice again, "Miss Foote, are you all right?"

All right! Such relief. It was only a bad dream. It must have been the crab casserole she had for dinner. Too rich and too late at night. Well, she's learned her lesson.

"I'm fine," she calls, "just a nightmare. So sorry to disturb you."

"All right then." She hears the landlady pad back down the hall.

She is drenched in sweat. She will have to get up and have a good wash. But all she really wants to do is simply lie here and count her blessings. However, even the sheets are soaked — she could take a chill.

Even the sheets are soaked. And Miss Foote realizes that in her terror of the dream she has wet herself — she has wet the bed. Like a small child or a very old person, her body has betrayed her. The power of the dream — which still does not seem so much a dream as a very real event from which she has only been saved by the landlady's knock — plus the humiliation of the wet bed, reduce Miss Foote to tears. She weeps as she hasn't wept in years, not since the day she walked into Daddy's study and found him on his knees, his forehead touching the floor like some worshipper of Allah, still alive but the victim of a stroke from which he never recovered. He had desperately tried to tell her something just before he died; she put her ear to his lips, but all that came out was a wheeze and something that sounded like "ice-cream," repeated three times, in between wheezes — "ice-cream, ice-cream, ice-cream."

"Ice-cream?" she had said, and the look in his eyes! The rage and fury and desperation. His message had not been understood.

And then he died and afterwards she wept.

What is she to do? What will Mrs Pelmet think of her? Will she tell the others? There is a launderette at the top of the village, near the car park, but it is closed on Sundays. That it is still Sunday and (she picks up the clock and yes, it is still ticking) only 8 A.M. is hard to believe. What to do?

Miss Foote gets out of bed, pulls off her sodden nightclothes and puts on her dressing gown. She can easily wash out her nightgown in the basement — she washes her smalls every night anyway and there is a clothesline in the back garden. But the sheet. And the mattress. She feels dizzy just thinking about it all. However, after she has washed her face and eaten an orange saved from the night before, she begins to pull herself together. She strips the bed and with considerable effort manages to turn the mattress and hide the large wet stain. It will dry eventually and Mrs Pelmet will, no doubt, never connect her, Agnes Foote, with the stain when she finally turns the mattress once more. Miss Foote rinses out the bottom sheet in cold water, wrings it out as best she can and stuffs it into the plastic carrier bag, which she hides at the back of her wardrobe. It will have to be dealt with tomorrow morning early. Then she makes up the bed with the remaining sheet, pulling the bedspread taut and arranging the pillows just so. She will tell Mrs Pelmet that as she'd been up so early she had decided to tidy her room herself. She has a leisurely bath, remembering not to have the water too hot, and gets dressed — comfortable skirt, blouse under her jumper in case she gets too warm while walking, stout shoes. She keeps her walking stick in the umbrella stand by the front door.

"Oh Miss Foote," cries the Honeymoon Girl, half of the Honeymoon Couple, "are you all right? You gave us such a fright, calling out like that!"

"Perfectly all right, thank you," says Miss Foote, taking her place at the breakfast table and helping herself to tea. Everyone looks at her expectantly; surely she is

going to tell them what she has been dreaming about.
Various theories have been advanced before she has
come down the stairs, some of them quite naughty. But
she says nothing, cuts up her bacon and egg and tomato
and eats without saying a word. And soon the topic
turns to other things: the disappearance of a baby, the
scandal of a millionaire who killed his wife, cut off her
head and kept the rest of the body in a sauna.

"For five months," cries Mrs Pelmet, who, when
everybody has been seen to, always sits down with her
guests and has a cup of tea. "He's pleading 'diminished
responsibility' — whatever do they mean by that?"

"Crazy when he did it," says the man from Reading.
"He says she taunted him, drove him to it. Teased him
about his" — here he looks around with a smile of
apology to the ladies — "his sexual prowess."

"Or lack of it," says the Honeymoon Boy. His bride
whispers something in his ear and he goes red as a
beetroot.

"Miss Foote," says the wife of the man from Reading,
"we are going to take a little drive this morning. To
Rock. We are planning to take the passenger ferry over
to Padstow and have a look round. Mrs Pelmet has kind-
ly made us a thermos of coffee. Would you like to join
us?

At this, Miss Foote comes out of her daze. She looks
around at the kind, inquiring faces. They are con-
cerned; they think she is ill and are trying to help. They
care. Courage comes back and warms her like a glass of
whiskey. Everything will be all right.

"Thank you so much," cries Miss Foote, "but I have
planned a walk to Port Quin this morning. Up the cliffs
and along the coast path. If Mrs Pelmet would be so
kind as to fill *my* thermos?"

Miss Foote gets up from the table. She is surprised to see that she has made a wreck of her piece of toast; torn bits and crumbs are scattered all around her plate. So silly to give in to nerves. A brisk walk is just the thing. She has a few digestive biscuits in her room and a Cadbury's bar. That, plus the coffee, will make a nice little picnic.

As she walks down the hill into the village and along to the west side, to Lobber Hill, where the path up to the cliffs begins, she smiles at one and all — the kiddies with their buckets and spades, the babies in push chairs, the elderly couple sitting on a bench. It is a beautiful day. "God's in His Heaven," she thinks, "all's right with the world." Was that Browning? "Pippa Passes"? Her memory isn't as good as it used to be. Browning had been one of her favourites. Such an elegant writer. And the love story, so romantic. She hums to herself as she strides through the narrow streets and starts up the hill.

The recorded church bells begin to ring as she starts her climb. And then, just as in the dream, they break off suddenly and the hymn begins:

Christ the Lord is Risen To-day-ay
A-ah-ah-ah-ah-lay-lew-oo-ya.

Miss Foote stops. She turns and stares down at the little harbour. The tide is out and the fishing boats are lying nearly on their sides. Through some trick of the wind she hears a man's impatient voice:

"No, no, Hilary, that's a *harbour*, not a holiday. We're *on* a holiday."

With one part of her mind Miss Foote thinks, "that child will never be allowed to grow up and be a poet."

She wonders which child it is, but is too far away to tell. Just one of the several little ones digging earnestly in the exposed sand. With another part of her mind she wills herself to turn and move bravely up the hill towards the dark figure she can see there, standing right in the middle of the path, reading the Sunday paper.

Local Customs

Local Customs

Years from now will he say to himself, "the breasts of that American girl had a bloom on them, like grapes." A combination of sun oil and the blowing sand, of course, but magic then, magic and terrifying to the twelve-year-old boy who was trying to look and not to look, both at the same time. Years from now will he perhaps rub his thumb and two fingers together and smile? As though he had actually touched them instead of merely staring across at her from his usual observation post under the dusty tamarisk tree. She and her friend are talking to the blind man, who lies propped on one elbow, on his suncot, not looking at either girl but somewhere off to one side. This has nothing to do with modesty; the blind man never looks at the people to whom he is talking. The wind and the fifteen yards between them keep Edward from hearing the conversation, but every so often he hears the blind man laugh and say "We Churmans, ha ha ha, we Churmans." His second day on the beach, Edward chased a newspaper which was blowing away in the wind. He brought the runaway pages to a middle-aged man, very tanned, who was sitting under one of the beach umbrellas. The paper was in German but Edward knew that most Germans spoke English. "Is this your paper?" he said, embarrassed by his high, thin, schoolboy voice. The man frowned in his direction.

"Bitte?"

"Your paper." Edward thrust it at the man.

"Ah, the newspaper. My wife's newspaper, I am afraid. I am blind."

Edward could just make out the shape of the man's eyes behind the thick dark glasses.

That day at lunch Anna said, "I wonder what's the matter with that man? It looks as though there's something wrong with his legs." Edward's father was reading a book, reaching absently for a forkful of salad from time to time. Edward took after his father; they were both long and thin and had the kind of skin that did not tan. Anna was his father's girlfriend.

"Who?" said Edward's father, not looking up.

"The German man over there, with the wife who is always smiling. She holds onto him — or rather, he holds onto her — wherever they go. She pretty well has to stand him up and sit him down."

"He's blind," Edward said. "He told me so this morning."

"Ah, so." Anna nodded her head at him and smiled. She had big white even teeth and was very pretty. Edward liked her in spite of himself. She was almost always willing to play cards or backgammon with him and she never called him Teddy, the way his mother did. ("Teddy's being so difficult lately," he heard her say, talking on the telephone to one of her friends. And then, "like father, like son.") And he knew Anna had nightmares. The walls between the rooms were thin and he had heard her crying out and moaning in the night. Edward knew a lot about bad dreams.

"His wife is Greek," Edward said, "but they've lived in Germany for years and years. She inherited a house in one of the villages, so they come here in the summer. They also have a house in Munich and a chalet in the Austrian alps."

"You are very good at finding things out," Anna said.

"Not really. He likes to talk."

And it was true — the blind man liked to talk. In English, in German, in bad Greek. From the time they arrived in the morning, his wife driving the white Mercedes, until they left in the late afternoon, the blind man lay on his suncot and talked to anyone who would listen. His wife, in a black bathing suit, her dark hair pulled into a low knot at the back of her neck, made trips across the beach and up to the café-bar for bottles of cold water and glasses of iced coffee. It was hard to tell how old she was, with her smooth brown skin and calm, untroubled face. She seemed to smile at everyone and had a special smile and greeting for Edward ever since he had rescued her newspaper. Twice a day she took her husband's hand and led him into the blue water, where they stood side by side up to their necks, facing the open sea for perhaps ten minutes. Then they turned and walked slowly back to their place under the beach umbrella. She handed him his towel and got him settled and went back for a swim on her own. She was a very strong swimmer and one day Edward had a strange thought. What if she got fed up looking after her husband and simply swam away?

In the last few days the wind has gotten worse. The umbrella man has stopped renting out umbrellas because the wind just knocks them out of their stands. "*Oxi*," he said, "no," shaking his head this morning at Edward, who likes to help with the umbrellas and cots, lining them up very early and then collecting the money from the people who want to rent them. One hundred drachmas for an umbrella, fifty drachmas each for a cot.

"*Kaputt*," the umbrella man says, "*verstehen?*"

"I'm *not German*," Edward insists, but the umbrella man ignores this and always addresses him as though he were. Although Edward knows perfectly well that there were good Germans and bad Germans during the Second World War it upsets him to actually be mistaken for one. Anna said once that she couldn't understand how the Greeks could bear to see a German without wanting to put a bullet through his head.

For three days now the wind has howled all night, rattling the louvred doors and windows in the hotel bedrooms, blowing sand into all the corners. A forest fire is raging in the north. All the young men from the northern villages have been conscripted to fight the fire. Big-bellied water bombers fly back and forth all day. Dmitri, Edward's friend who owns the hotel and café-bar, tells him that some of the islanders are saying it was the tourists who caused the fire but that this isn't true. Last year's fire was started by an old man burning brush in his field and this year's was probably caused by lightning.

"Or maybe the government starts it, who knows?"

Edward does not understand. Dmitri likes him because he collects all the empty bottles from the beach and generally makes himself useful. Dmitri doesn't mind Edward asking him questions.

"Why would the government start a fire?"

"Take people's mind from politics, from troubles."

Edward still doesn't understand. It is a small island; sometimes, in the evenings, you can smell the forests burning in the north. The sunsets are spectacular.

Empty containers for Manhattan Ice-Cream, Tartuffo Gelato Italiano, Coke bottles, Sprite bottles, Pizz lemonade, beer, water bottles, Marlboro packets: during the night the wind sweeps all the rubbish into heaps against the low stone wall which separates the beach from the café and the parking lot in front of the small hotel. By 7:00 A.M. Edward has had his first swim of the day and is sorting through the rubbish. If he finds bits of broken glass, or bottle caps, he places them carefully in a plastic bag.

"You good boy," Dmitri says, "maybe you no go back to England. You stay here with me."

Dmitri isn't married. Everybody thinks, at first, that his sister Fotula is his wife. It is really Fotula who owns the place; property here is passed on to the daughters, not the sons. Dmmi, as his friends and family call him, spent five years working in restaurants in New Jersey and Montreal, living in cheap boarding houses and sending money back so that Fotula could build the thirteen-room hotel. In return she sent him photographs of how the work was coming on. Anna has the pink card which advertises the hotel pasted in her diary:

NEAR BEACH RESTAURANT
PERA AMMOS
IF YOU ENJOY SWIMMING AND PINETREES
SURROUNDING IS NO BETTER PLACE

Dmmi and Fotula wear T-shirts made for them by a

satisfied client. PERA AMMOS they say, GOLDEN
SANDS BEACH RESORT. On the glass case in front of
the bar are a lot of pictures of Dmmi in his T-shirt, with
his arm around various pretty girls. He says to Edward,
"You think I should make new T-shirt? 'Fotula is no my
wife'?" He is a handsome dark-haired man of about
forty-five. At least Anna says he is handsome; Edward
notices he is getting a fat belly.

The whole family works at one job or another about
the place. No matter how early Edward arrives with his
sack of bottles, the old granny, the *yia yia*, is already sitting on a straight chair on one side of the door to the
kitchen, stuffing tomatoes or green peppers, stringing
beans. The old grandpa sits on the other side peeling
an enormous pan of potatoes. Dmitri and Fotula's older
brother, who is a bit simple, sweeps up and waits on
tables. A handsome nephew runs the gift shop and even
the umbrella man is some sort of relation. The older
brother and his wife, who is the chambermaid, have
two naughty children who are alternately kissed and
slapped. They hold up the wet sheets for their mother
to hang on the line, and fall asleep, in the evenings, on
their granny's lap.

Edward is an only child. Since the divorce, his
parents never speak to one another except over the
telephone, and his grandparents live in distant cities.
He has already been a boarder at school for three years.

"You think I should get a wife?" Dmitri says to
Edward one day. "Maybe nice English womans?" They
are busy setting out chairs and wiping down tables.
Edward smiles but doesn't answer. If he had thought
Dmitri was Fotula's husband, Dmitri had thought Anna
was Edward's older sister. He had shown them to the
same room. Anna had thought this was very funny.

On the beach an Englishman walks by; he is big and boisterous and wears a black T-shirt with CATS printed on one side, two green cat's eyes on the other. "I say," he calls to no one in particular, certainly not to the boy, for Edward has seen this man has no time for children, "crossing the beach in this wind is like crossing the Gobi Desert!" He is a stupid man with a stupid wife and two stupid daughters. The girls parade around in just their bikini bottoms and are dreadful show-offs. Their breasts have just begun to swell. One has nipples the colour of field mushrooms; the other's are dusty pink, like pencil rubbers. They play frisbee and a game involving two large plastic bats and a tennis ball; they stand at the water's edge each afternoon, squealing and hoping everybody is looking at them, flinging their arms around and missing perfectly easy throws. Edward watches them from the shade of the tamarisk tree. One day they asked him to play and when he shook his head and hurried away they laughed.

"We Churmans," the blind man says, "ha ha ha." He is passing around photographs of his houses.

It is hard to know where to look. Although there is a sign in Greek, English, German and Italian which says NUDITY IS FORBIDDEN, many women are barebreasted. And some of the Greek women are very fat. They look terrible in their two-piece suits, their stomachs spilling over in yellowish rolls. Some have dreadful scars and he doesn't see how they can expose themselves like that, talking away to one another, shouting at their children, passing out food. The little Greek boys fill empty Pizz bottles with sea-water and run along the shore, pouring out the water in long streams, shouting "Pizz, pizz" and laughing.

But the other beach is much worse. On the other

beach, the beach where Anna and Edward's father go, everyone is stark naked — man, woman and child. Anna knew about the other beach before they came; she has been to this island once before. On their first day, after the business about the rooms had been sorted out and they had unpacked, Anna said, "Come with me and I will show you the most beautiful beach in the world." She led them up a path along the steep cliffs beyond the bay. They walked for about ten minutes and then she started down towards the water. They followed, slipping and sliding behind her, not always sure where to put their feet, until they came out on a small beach covered in smooth grey pebbles, as though they had stumbled upon a gigantic nest of stone eggs. A hundred yards from shore two men, completely naked, were diving from a large rock. "And now," Anna said, spreading her towel over the smooth, round pebbles, "now we take off our clothes and let the sun shine all over us." She was unbuttoning her skirt as she spoke. Soon she and his father had shed all their clothes, their bodies very pale compared to the few other people lying on the beach or swimming in the blue-green water.

"Come on Teddy," his father said, "it's all right. Anna says we're allowed to swim nude over here. Off with your clothes. You look as though you could do with a bit of sunshine."

Nude. It rhymed with rude. What an ugly word.

Anna stood smiling at him. "It feels so nice; why don't you give it a try?"

"In a minute," he said. He spread out his towel and carefully anchored it at the corners with large grey stones.

Anna and his father lay down side by side, faces to the sun, holding hands.

"Aren't you glad we came?" she asked. She leaned over and kissed his father on the belly. His father's cock stirred and thickened. Edward went quickly to the water's edge, pulled off his shorts and ran into the water. The rocks were slippery here and he fell once or twice but was quickly over his head.

When Anna had stood there smiling at him she was wearing only the necklace of blue beads his father had bought her in Athens. For their "anniversary" he had said. The man in the shop swore they were genuine mummy beads and now Edward, swimming, remembered the Mummy Room at the British Museum and one mummy in particular. The brownish bandages covering the body were covered in turn by a broken net of blue beads. Where did the jeweller in Athens get his? From men who robbed tombs? It seemed strange to him, as he floated on his back in the cool water, the sun so hot against his closed eyes, that Anna would want to wear something like that, something that had been shut up in a tomb for hundreds and hundreds of years, maybe something that had a curse on it.

Edward had been on a school tour of the museum and the guide had told them all about curses connected with the tombs. When they were going through from one hall to another there had been a marble statue of a girl, a goddess maybe, lying on her stomach, asleep. One of the boys pretended to stick his finger up her bum when the guard wasn't looking.

When Edward came out of the water he quickly

wrapped himself in his towel and moved away from Anna and his father.

He went one more time to the pebble beach and sat in the shade of the cliff. A French couple came to share the shade and the woman showed him an angry red circle on her arm. "*La méduse*," she said, "*attention!*" Edward was surprised that anyone would think he was French. Her husband was wearing only the top of his wetsuit and had been spearing fish. When Edward looked puzzled (what was a *méduse?*) he said, "jelay-fish" then turned his back and began talking to his wife in rapid French.

After that Edward said he preferred the sandy beach by the hotel. For a moment he thought his father was angry. Then he shrugged. "It's up to you. We can join you at lunchtime. If you need anything, just put it on the bill." And so their routine was quickly established. Edward stayed on the sandy beach; he helped Dmitri and the umbrella man; he swam; he watched. Sometimes he ate lunch with his father and Anna. Sometimes he helped Dmitri and his brother wait on tables. Lunch was their busiest time, for the buses had arrived from the town by then, and the people in cars and young men riding motor scooters or hanging on behind the driver. The beach filled up and everybody wanted beer or Sprite or Pizz, salad, moussaka, fish and chips, ice-cream and iced coffee. One day Dmitri asked him to take an order to the family with the English girls and he refused. Dmitri laughed.

"What's the matter? They your girlfriends?"

Edward shook his head, furious. He went back to his room and lay on his bed until lunchtime was almost over. Anna, worried that he'd had too much sun,

brought him a big plate of watermelon and played
Snap with him until the sun was lower in the sky. His
father sat on the adjoining balcony reading a book and
when he suggested they all go to the other taverna,
about ten minutes away and in the opposite direction
to the pebbly beach, Edward, who had always refused
before out of loyalty to Dmitri, agreed at once. Anna
and his father liked the other taverna better in the evenings. It was lively and cooler and often had local musicians. The evening was pleasant and they stayed late,
walking back along the cliffs. A girl had fallen from the
path and onto the rocks a few weeks before. She had
been drunk and there was no moon. A German girl.
Edward thought of her lying there in the darkness, her
head split open like a watermelon, and watched very
carefully where he put his feet.

And the next day Dmitri offered to show him some
card tricks so they were friends again.

"So how you like this ice-land," Dmitri said, shuffling
the cards. Edward shook his head, puzzled. "Karpathos,
how you like it?"

"Eye-land," Edward corrected him, "this eye-land."

On the beach Greek-American women changed from
one language to another in the middle of a sentence.
"Okay, *pethi mou*, now you're really going to get it!"
Switching the backs of their children's legs with narrow
bamboo fishing poles. Edward was learning, slowly, but
the air was full of words he didn't understand. He tried
to imagine Dmmi learning English in Elizabeth, New
Jersey.

One morning when Edward went down to arrange his
things in his favourite spot under the tamarisk tree, a

young man was there, curled up in a cotton sleeping bag. Edward wasn't sure what to do. He felt that this was his spot, although he knew that it wasn't, not really. He also knew that if he didn't arrange his things now, before he had breakfast, somebody else would come along and claim it. The tree provided shade all day and you didn't have to pay for an umbrella. And the whole beach was there in front of him, like a continuous film. As he stood there, undecided, the young man turned over and opened his eyes.

"Good morning," he said. He was German. "I am taking your place?"

Edward shrugged. "Not really. But I like it here under the tree. I don't tan very well," he confessed.

The young man sat up and the sleeping bag fell back around his waist. He laughed.

"I also. I do not tan very well." He showed Edward his back. "Yesterday I fall asleep in the sun. Now I am all burned up." When he stepped out of the sleeping bag, the backs of his legs were bright red.

"You could get sunstroke," Edward said. "You should be careful."

The man nodded. "Yah. I drank some beer and I fall asleep. Very dumb."

"Where were you?"

"On the other beach, mit the rocks."

"Where are you staying?"

"I have a little tent," he said. "I am staying on the beaches mostly. But the wind is too strong and pulls it down, my tent. And the sun is very hot."

"You should stay out of the sun today," Edward said, "or you will get sick." He offered him one side of the shade from the tree.

The man went to shave and wash up in the public

washroom and Edward went for his breakfast. Anna and his father were still asleep. The only people in the café were Dmitri and the old granny and grandpa and the couple Anna called "the newly-weds," although the girl didn't wear a wedding ring. She was taking a picture of her boyfriend eating yoghurt and honey. She was always taking pictures of her boyfriend or he of her. "James Hooper," he said to her now, posing, "this is your life."

The young German asked if he could join Edward for breakfast. Edward said yes, but added he had to hurry and help the umbrella man set out the cots and umbrellas. The man nodded and smiled. Edward liked the way he looked right at you.

"*Kalli-mara,*" Dmitri said to Edward, "*Tee-kanees?*"

"*Kalla,*" Edward replied.

"You speak Greek?" the young man said to Edward.

"A little."

They spent the day together, under the tamarisk tree. The young man's name was Karl. He was tall and thin, with reddish hair and pale blue eyes. He seemed always to be wearing a slight frown but he had a nice smile. He had a degree in psychology, he said, but couldn't get a job, so he was selling potatoes in a shop in Berlin.

"I am very bad. Some ladies come in and they want very cheap potatoes, not much money, and some are wanting very expensive potatoes, high class, and I always forget what lady wants what potatoes. I am not a very good potato-seller."

Edward told him a little about his school and where he lived in Sussex and a little about his father and Anna, although he said "my father and stepmother" which was what she was, really, and it sounded nicer.

"Are you married?" he said.

"Me? I am too shy. Someday maybe."

The German was travelling alone. He was very well organized and had only his small rucksack and tent and cotton sleeping bag. Edward's father and Anna made fun of the Americans with their enormous packs. "Life-support systems," they called them. They would approve of the way this man travelled so lightly.

"I bring only — what you call them — necessaries," he said. "But a book of course. One book. However, even with one book I am not very far." It was a very fat paperback, *Gravity's Rainbow.*

"What's it about?" Edward asked.

"The wars," the young man said.

Edward thought he said "divorce."

"But I am not in the mood for reading. I like to watch. For example," he said, smiling, "you notice how the women lie when they lie on the beach. Always with one leg up, only one, like so," and he bent his right leg into a triangle. "And the mothers, they are always calling so loudly to their children, do this, don't do that. And the young girls are always rubbing each other with oil." He showed Edward a small black notebook in which he wrote down what he saw. Edward told him about the "newly-weds" who were always taking pictures and about all the Greeks from New Jersey.

"Yah. On this island most all the men go away to make money. They send money back. They come back to visit, to die. They fix up the villages."

They were going to a village that night, Edward said, to a festival. They were being picked up by a taxi. He wanted to invite his new friend to come with them but wasn't sure how Anna and his father would feel about that. Dmitri's handsome nephew was supposed to be minding the gift shop but instead was showing off with a friend of his, a young man in a white panama hat, for some Greek-American girls. They had a tape-recorder going full blast.

"'Beat it'," the young German said, laughing. "'Beat it'. You like Michael Jackson? You like to dance?"

Edward shrugged. The blind man's wife came across the beach in her black bathing suit. She smiled her special smile.

"And how are you today?" she said.

"Everybody knows you," his new friend said, admiringly. It made Edward feel good to hear him say it.

That evening they arrived early at the mountain village because Anna wanted to be up there when the sun set. Edward had sat in front with the taxi driver, whose name was Adonis. He had a horn that played "My Old Kentucky Home." The air was very cool and they sat on a stone wall, outside the church, waiting for the procession to begin. Anna wore an embroidered shawl over her sundress and looked very beautiful. But Edward's father became impatient when he discovered the procession wouldn't start for some time and suggested they go for a walk. So they walked away from the village, past grape-vines and terraces of olive trees, past a house where two small children were being coached in the dancing by a mama and a proud grandpa. And further along a very new, very black baby goat showed off for them while its mother calmly ate her dinner. Anna and Edward's father walked with their arms around one another; Edward dropped a little behind. The sunset turned the stone terraces, the fields, their faces, the whole sky golden, then rose, then a deep orangey-red. Somewhere a group of musicians were playing the strange, mournful, repetitive music they had heard before at the other taverna on the beach. Edward said it reminded him of bees and his father smiled at him. "That's a very interesting perception."

Walking back to the main village they came upon the musicians entering a house. "They will go from house to house tonight and make up songs to honour the people," Anna said. She had been reading the guidebook. A little further on, through an open doorway, Edward saw a man in a brown suit, humming to himself, select a gaudy tie from an open chest of drawers.

The taverna, which was famous for its home-made sausages, was jammed with people. The proprietor's son, not much older than Edward, was very busy laying plastic tablecloths, bringing baskets of bread, bottles of retsina and beer, plates of the famous sausages. The blind man and his wife were sitting with a large group. When she saw Edward, the blind man's wife, in a full red skirt and red blouse, her hair braided into a crown on top of her head, got up from the table and came across the room. She gave Edward and his father and Anna each a sprig of wild thyme.

"It is the custom here," she said, "on feast days."

"If there were some instrument to measure happiness," Anna said, "I'm sure that mine, tonight, would break it."

"Anna," Edward's father said, "will you do me the honour of marrying me?"

Edward saw his friend, the young German, over in a corner reading his book. They smiled and waved.

"Another new friend?" Edward's father said.

"He has a degree in clinical psychology," Edward said, "but has to sell potatoes in Berlin."

"Isn't he wonderful?" Anna said. "Edward, would you do me the honour of marrying me?"

One morning very early Edward and Karl walked over the cliffs and all the way into the town. Karl showed him how to find the path even when it didn't look as though there was one and how there were small heaps of stone every so often, "little stone men" Karl called them, when the path made a sudden turn, and splashes of red paint. Karl needed to find out when boats were leaving for Crete. He had to be in Athens on a certain day to get his flight back to Berlin. He really wanted to take an old boat that went all the way to Piraeus but nobody knew exactly when it would arrive and nobody knew where he could get a ticket. "Dmmi says it is a very funny boat," Karl told Edward, "but when I say how funny he just laughs." Instead of his usual singlet or khaki shirt Karl was wearing a blue shirt covered in bright flowers. It made him look quite different. "You like it?" Karl said. "I wear it for the very first time."

Edward imagined himself, in a few years, travelling from place to place with his rucksack on his back.

The walk along the cliffs took just over an hour and they watched the sun rise as they walked along. The air smelled of wild thyme and oregano. They passed a field of oats, golden in the morning light.

"So sometimes I am thinking we are in the Bible," Karl said.

In town they had a Nescafé at the port and then visited the bank, the travel agent, the post office, a vegetable shop where they bought round yellow melons and grapes, a shop that sold yoghurt, one that sold nuts and spirits. Everything fit neatly into Karl's rucksack.

Anna had asked Edward to try and match some embroidery silk. They found a shop with hundreds of boxes of silks and cottons, and with the aid of the proprietor, a very old man, they were able to match the sample exactly. The shop had a painted fish on a sign outside the door and it also sold fishing equipment — fishing line and sinkers, fishnet, flippers, masks. Karl, who had a snorkelling outfit, offered to buy one for Edward. That afternoon they took their gear to the pebble beach and went snorkelling in the deep water. Edward was amazed to find that he could see right through the bodies of some of the fish. Sometimes they brushed against his mask; sometimes they brushed against his body or swam between his legs. Karl, who was swimming alongside him, warned him away from a group of what looked like pale purple bubbles. Back on the beach, drying off, he told Edward they were jellyfish. Edward remembered the French woman and her warning about the *méduse*.

Anna came over to where they were sitting and asked to borrow the mask and snorkel. Edward's flippers were too small; Karl's were too big. She stood there, smiling, swinging the mask and talking to the young man. She was a soft brown all over and wore nothing but the blue and silver necklace.

Edward noticed how, when the water ran over the shingle as it flowed back into the sea, it made a hissing sound.

The blind man lies on his suncot and laughs — "Ha ha ha, we Churmans, ha ha ha." Edward, tired of sitting still, wishing Anna were there so he could show her his latest card trick, gets up, picks up his snorkelling equipment and goes down to the water.

Edward sees the octopus first. As the crowd gathers, he keeps repeating it: "I'm the one that found it!" He wishes Anna and his father would come back.

He had been snorkelling for about an hour and as he came in towards the beach he kept his face down in the water until the last minute, until he was almost lying on the sand. That was when a clump of something swam between his mask and the edge of the shore. Whatever it was had brushed against his cheek and he stood up in a panic. It was a small octopus, the tips of its tentacles curling and uncurling, just under the surface of the water. Perhaps it had hurt itself when it collided with his mask. Edward knelt down in the water to have a better look. The young man in the panama hat was walking by. His green-and-white striped swimming trunks were much too tight and now he stood above Edward, smiling.

"What you got?"

Edward didn't like the young man but he was too excited to keep quiet and ignore him.

"It's an octopus! It crashed right into my mask! Do you think it's hurt?"

"*Otopothi*," the young man said, squatting down. "Very nice to eat." He gave it a poke with his finger and the tentacles curled in upon themselves like strange warty fingers, like the tips of young ferns. Its eyes were shut tight. The young man laughed. He wore a large gold cross on a gold chain. His chest, his belly, his legs were covered in whorls of coarse black hair.

"Very nice to eat. I show you." He reached down

quickly and picked up the creature. Now the tentacles twisted around the young man's hand. He offered the octopus to Edward.

"You like? I show you how to fix. Dmmi cook it for you." The tentacles curled, uncurled (*"la méduse, attention!"*). Edward put his hands behind his back.

The man in the panama hat laughed, showing glints of gold among his strong white teeth.

"You no like?"

Edward hesitated. A small crowd had gathered. The young man laughed again and called to two of his friends. He said something in Greek and they laughed and came forward. Edward wondered what it would be like to grab the octopus and run with it, drop it in the blind man's lap. Would the blind man's wife stop smiling, then?

The three young men moved out a bit into the water, forming a loose triangle. The man in the hat let the octopus go and they began to play with it, scooting it through the water towards one another, standing up to their knees in water, laughing. Edward stood near but not too near, watching. The octopus was frantic now; it turned an ugly red and squirted its ink at the young men. Their legs were covered in it and this made them laugh even harder. The man in the panama hat called something to two pretty Greek girls and rubbed the black stuff into the skin of his thighs. The girls giggled.

As more and more people joined the crowd Edward called out, "I'm the one that found it! It crashed right into my mask!" But still he stood at the edge of the game, in his flippers, holding the mask and snorkel. He wanted to touch the octopus, to hold it, maybe get somebody to take a photograph. He could see the "newly-weds" in the crowd; the girl, as usual, had her camera on a cord around her wrist. He could see the English girls, who had left off making an elaborate sand castle and stood there, shameless, their little titties sticking out for everybody to see. But the idea of really holding the thing made him feel sick. The way it would twist and turn, curl and uncurl against his hand. It was horrible to think about, horrible to look at, boneless, like a wrinkled purse made of skin. Big ones could kill a man. What if there were big ones out there, under the cliffs where he'd been swimming? The afternoon sun beat down on the back of his neck.

The man in the panama hat was tired of the game. He scooped up the octopus and looked around for Edward.

"You sure you no like? Very nice to eat." (Surprising his father and Anna at dinner that night. "Dmmi cooked something special. I caught it.") He shook his head.

"Okay. Thank you for my supper." The man in the hat began to walk to the far side of the beach, where the rocks were. The crowd broke up. Edward took his flippers off and followed at a distance, walking just at the edge of the water.

When the man got to the rocks he began slapping the octopus against the rocks, very hard. The first blow must have killed it. Slap, slap — it sounded like wet wash against a rock, like wet towels. In the showers at school, sometimes the prefects would slap the younger boys with towels. Slap. Slap. It was horrible, beastly. Why hadn't he swum back out with it and let it go? Edward knew what he was doing; he'd seen the fishermen sometimes, early in the morning, slapping octopus against the rocks and his German friend had explained why they did this. "We are pounding the veal," he said, "they are pounding the octopus." He had given Edward his address in Berlin. "Maybe someday you will come and see me." Edward wished Karl was there right now. He'd know what to do.

The man in the panama hat walked back along the beach, the dead octopus draped over his arm, the tentacles hanging down, not twisting now, limp, harmless.

One of the pretty Greek girls called to him and he stopped. While Edward watched the young man tore off a tentacle and threw it to the girl. She caught it, ("bravo, bravo" called the man in the panama hat), wound it around her wrist like some horrible bracelet, smiled and went on talking to her friend.

The two stupid English girls had gone up to the café for ice-cream or drinks. Their mother and father were asleep in their suncots farther along the beach. Edward, who was now very familiar with the kitchen of Dmitri and Fotula, thought that the mother's skin was turning the colour of a cockroach. He put on his flippers and glancing around to make sure no one was looking, he quickly stamped the sandcastle into the ground. Served them right. Then he turned and walked backwards, went into the sea. He wet his mask, spit on it, rubbed the spit around. He put the mask on, bit the mouthpiece of the snorkel, turned away from the beach and began to swim. He tried not to think about the dead octopus, about the tentacle torn off and draped over the girl's arm or the possibility of others out there somewhere, waiting.

And that night he has a strange dream. He is on one of the turquoise and cream buses, going into the port. There is a young man on the bus and perhaps an older man who isn't feeling very well. He turns around in his seat and in the seat behind Edward sees a Greek girl holding an octopus in her lap. He thinks, "now I will get to see the colour of its eyes." He suggests to the girl that she tickle it so that its eyes will open. She does this and it looks right at him — its eyes are a bright, bright blue. Then it begins to turn into a baby, quite a pretty round-faced baby, and it smiles. But as it opens its mouth wider Edward can see that as well as having a mouth and lips it has a hole, like a large siphon, at the back of its throat. It is very round, this hole, and fleshy, and the edges are moving slightly in and out.

Edward wakes up to the sound of Anna crying out in the other room.

The Dance

The Dance

This past summer, at the Disco Romantika, I realized that I am what used to be referred to as "on the shelf." Temporarily, let us hope, for what is "on the shelf" now can presumably be taken off at some later date, like a jar of preserves sealed up in August to be enjoyed in the chilly days of winter. It is then that we reach down into one of these jars and what bursts upon the tongue, is it not all the more astonishing for being sampled out of season? Does it not recall the very essence of those bee-laden, scented days? Or so I tell myself, deriving a little comfort from this pretty metaphor. Unfortunately, the real facts of fruit shut up in a jar recall another expression, one of those kiss/slap remarks made by one person, usually a woman, about another: "She's very well preserved for her age." I won't think about that or about "shelf-life" or about items in supermarkets labelled "best before_____" with a date stamped in.

Instead, let us get back to the Disco Romantika. I can hardly get away from it, lying here in the darkness with the sliding door to the balcony partly open and the sounds from the Disco coming faint but insistent across the quarter-mile (if that) which separates it from our bungalow.

> She works hard for the money
> (she works hard for the money)
> She works hard for her honey
> (she works hard for her honey)

The coloured lights revolve in their semi-circles, blue/red/green/yellow, set in a bar like some strange traffic signal. (If red means stop and green means go, what do you suppose that blue means?) The lights leave rich transparent circles on the dancers, the marble dance floor, the jetting fountains, whose spouts are the gilded mouths of baby angels or of Eros, their faces turned upwards to the starry sky. For the Disco Romantika is open-air and that is one of the interesting things about it — all that changing and shifting light, all that motion and commotion down below while the stars carry on their fixed dance up above.

"Po-Mantika," my daughter scoffs, the first time we pass it on our way into the town. It is daylight and the sign is not lit up. From the outside, the place doesn't look very interesting at all. A couple of brown hens are pecking in the dirt just outside the entrance and we can hear somebody inside sweeping up bits of broken crockery.

"They just wrote a Greek R," I say; "you can see how easily it could happen. It was probably too expensive to get fixed. Or maybe one of the legs dropped off."

"Hmmph," she says. She is not in the best of moods.

We are walking into town in order to have a look
around, in order to explore, in order to find out about
bus schedules to some of the villages we have read
about, in order to escape from Bungalows Limenos
where we have the misfortune to be staying. My
daughter is in a scoffing mood. We have left a perfectly
wonderful island where we were having a perfectly
wonderful time — she has already forgotten about the
flies, the wasps who hovered greedily over her breakfast
of yoghurt and honey, the heat so terrific that we
banned all active verbs, such as "walk," after 11 A.M. —
to come to this pretentious, ridiculous, *boring* place, and
all because her mother felt they should see more of
Greece than one small island in the southern Aegean.
But as she has so rightly pointed out, there is nothing
very Greek about Bungalows Limenos except the
manager, the waiters and the chambermaids. We could
be anywhere that boasts blue water and a sandy beach.

"Let's go to the disco some night soon," I say, trying
to cheer her up.

She shrugs her shoulders. "Maybe."

We flew up here, after a thirty-seven-hour ferry ride, and
a night at a pension in Athens. I think now this was a
mistake, the flying up. We are going back from Kavalla
to Athens by bus but we should have done it the other
way around. The plane went up; an hour later it came
down. A combination Pegasus and Trojan Horse, it
disgorged its army of tourists and swallowed up
another. My daughter has no sense of how the landscape changes as one moves north or why, as we sped
along in a taxi from the airport to the place where we
would board a ferry to the island, she felt that "it
doesn't look like Greece." Her Greece has been either

the noisy bustle of Athens or the landscape of that other island, its hills so sparsely tufted they reminded one from a distance of worn-out upholstery, its pastel houses clinging to the hills like barnacles. Not this — not all this *green*, not field after field of corn and not hibiscus blossoms and frangipani. I thought it looked like California.

"Well it sure doesn't look like *Greece*," she repeated. "I can't believe this."

The enormous car-ferry to the island was crowded with holiday-makers, none of them speaking English, but there was an old Barbara Stanwyck movie on the T.V. in the lounge. Barbara was managing oil rigs (not inappropriately, I thought, for they are drilling for oil up here in the northern Aegean) and talking back to men in that sexy voice she has. We bought iced coffees and took them up on deck, where we sat watching the island come towards us. I like going places by boat; I suppose it has something to do with "crossing the waters," which to me is always symbolic as well as real. At first the boat is very large and whatever you are heading for invisible or just a smudge on the horizon. Gradually the smudge becomes larger and larger until there is a moment when the boat and the island appear to be the same size. That is a wonderful moment, for me. It is like the moment before the tide turns, when the whole universe seems to be in balance. The island is there all right, it's real, you didn't get on the wrong boat by mistake (see, everyone up here is breathing its name — Bulgarians, Yugoslavians, Germans, Greeks, Italians) but you don't, yet, have to do anything, gather up packs, check for wallet or purse, put away the *Blue*

Guide. One of the delights of this summer has been the discovery that this daughter who looks for all the world like the epitome of "The Pepsi Generation" or "Gidget goes to Greece," loves to travel on boats. I thought she might get impatient, but I was wrong. She has decided that she likes the whole sense of "getting there" and is willing to wait for "there" while she enjoys the voyage. It has created a great bond between us. As we approached the island and began our descent to the car deck, we noticed posters advertising various discos in and around the port. One of these was for the Disco Romantika, although we didn't realize that until later. We laugh at the sign under a fire axe: "BRAKE GLASS."

Bungalows Limenos is beautiful to look at. A broad asphalt road curves down from the reception building towards a long beach of white sand. Branching off from this main road are small paths covered in pine needles. These lead to various "bungalows," which are really a series of beautifully designed rooms, each with bath and balcony, usually attached to one another in groups of four. There are flowers everywhere and hedges and long-needled pines and low stone walls. The hedges glisten and the smell of the flowers is almost overpowering, like a florist's shop.

"It's been raining," my daughter says as we step around a few puddles, following the boy who has insisted on carrying our luggage. We have just come from an island where it has not rained for five months.

"I expect the gardeners have been watering the flowers," I say. It is certainly cooler here, pleasantly so. I can actually imagine doing some exploring, taking walks, climbing to the acropolis up above the town.

And the room is beautiful, spacious, with a grey and white marble floor, comfortable beds, a real bathroom with a real tub, instead of a communal shower and toilet with goats peering in the window. This was style, this was class. We look up the times for meals (we are required to take half board) and then, as the navigator who has managed to get us from way down in the south to way up in the north without incident or accident or loss of portable property, I take a nap while my daughter goes to the beach for a swim.

After that first dreamless sleep, things go rapidly downhill. The "attractive dining-room" turns out to be more like a dining-hall in some enormous summer camp. The place is full of families with young children, all of them under twelve. Because the walls of the dining-room are concrete, the din is terrible. Cacophony is a good Greek word. Have you ever been to a big indoor swimming pool on a Saturday after-noon? The effect is something like that. And all the grown-ups talking away as well, talking loudly. The headwaiter, who is dressed very curiously in an outfit that makes him look Mexican, not Greek, shows us to a table and commandeers a waiter to attend us. He does this not by snapping his fingers, but by pursing his lips and making a long kissing sound and then calling the man's name. Most of the waiters are young but ours is not. He speaks to us in German. I say that we do not speak German, we speak English. It soon becomes ob-vious that his English is very limited and he would prefer it if we spoke Greek or German. During our stay he speaks to us in German whenever he sees us and his manner seems to indicate that he believes we really can speak German and are only trying to make his life more difficult than it already is. I tell him he can speak in

Greek and if he speaks slowly ("sigha, sigha") I will probably understand. For reasons best known to himself he doesn't want to do this and stumbles along in English or rattles away in German. Never mind, his descriptions of the menu wouldn't have made much difference. In spite of the brochure, which has called our attention to "international dishes" and *"haute cuisine"* that it was going to be our delight to sample, the food is terrible. *Terrible.* With all the abundance of fruit and vegetables, of lamb, of everything delicious on the island, it is a perverse miracle that the food can be so bad. The entrée at dinner is often a big chunk of stringy mutton in gravy, resembling nothing so much as a lump of soft rock plucked out of a mudslide, with mud-looking vegetables to accompany it. The comical part is that the waiters, who, as we learned later, have all been to "tourist school," bend low over fake-silver platters or soup tureens, serving or ladling out this awful food in a manner that would do credit to a five-star restaurant anywhere in the world. That is the comical part. What is unfunny is that we have to pay for two meals a day whether we eat them or not.

"I can't eat this," my daughter said.

"You'll eat it," I said. "We'll both eat it."

"I can't." She pushed the food around her plate but only ate an enormous slice of watermelon for dessert.

"Maybe it's an off day," I suggested. (But alas, it wasn't.)

The next day plunged us even deeper into gloom. Clouds had been building up from about ten o'clock on and by two-thirty it was pouring. The rain never let up except briefly, around five P.M., and then it began again. Our umbrella was with our friends in Athens, along with things marked "needed for London." And it was chilly. We lay on our beds reading trash books and thinking up silly ways to get kicked out of the place. Breakfast had been the Greek equivalent of Tang plus slices of cake or bread and coffee. It cost sixty-five drachmas extra to have an egg and, although when our waiter said "drie minuti?" I shook my head and held up five fingers, he came back almost immediately with two very soft-boiled eggs, the kind neither of us can stand, the kind you give to babies, dipping in little pieces of bread when they are first beginning to eat solid food, opening your mouth wide saying yum yum. It was sixty-five drachmas extra for yoghurt, and on an island famous for its honey we were given imported packets of jam or marmalade to have with our bread and cake. For lunch we ate fruit and nuts we had brought with us and then it began to rain. We could not face dinner, in the rain, in the dining-room. I had seen in the brochure — not that I trusted it any more — that there was a taverna somewhere on the grounds. At eight o'clock I decided we should try and find it. My daughter was surprised.

"I thought you said we had to eat the meals here because we can't get out of paying for them."

"There are times," I said, "when morale is more important than money" and off we went into the rain.

We found the taverna — we were the only customers — and ate a good meal of *souvlaki, tzatziki*, chips and wine. A family ran the place and the oldest boy said that the disco was very good, we should try it. He also told us the sun would shine the next day and it did. We spent most of the day on the beach and discovered, with the return of the warm weather, that tables had been laid in the courtyard outside the dining-hall. The food was still awful and we had to pay sixty-five drachmas extra to get feta cheese and olives on our "Greek" salad but the noise level was improved by eating out in the open.

It really was a "family" resort. There were one or two honeymoon couples and a trio of English girls in their twenties, two very pretty and one very plain. But mostly there were families. On the beach I watched the families — father, mother, and one or two kids — talking, playing, exchanging information and commands the way families do, and I felt very strange. There is no rule that says a family has to have a father, but there is a strange convention with families on holidays, that unless the holiday consists of going to a family cottage, a father should be in evidence. Even if it is actually the mother who makes all the plans and reservations, does the packing, cancels the milk and arranges for the mail, even if it is really the mother who is *in charge*, the father should be there. We were not a honeymoon couple nor two young secretaries on a holiday — we did not somehow "fit in." I had not felt this before in Greece. Indeed, five years before I had been on a beach in Crete with not just one but three daughters and no one had thought it strange. Everyone was very friendly to us — *Kalli-mara*, good morning, they would call when they saw us coming. I wore a black bathing suit then; perhaps they thought I was a widow. And of course I am talking about Greeks, and particularly about Greek women. The older ones know a great deal about young widows — they have watched husbands and sons being lined up against walls and shot. Now I wear a turquoise bathing suit and of course there are no Greeks or none that I can see. On this beach I simply do not count. It is not just the language barrier — the family next to me that first morning were speaking French and my French isn't bad — it was another kind of barrier. These people did not need anyone else, unless it were another family with children who would play together happily with theirs. There was one teenager, a beautiful Italian girl, but she was with her family *and* a friend. I could almost hear my daughter thinking what she was too polite to say aloud. "At this time, on the other island, I would have been — " For she had made friends quickly and easily there, with a group of Greek boys and girls, and had had a wonderful time.

And so we began to walk into the town, to explore, to climb the acropolis, to take buses to small villages. One day, in the local museum, I pointed out to my daughter a Roman statue of Nemesis, or Fate. She had wings still but her head was missing and one arm.

"Look," I said, "even Fate is not impervious to Fate. There is a destiny which shapes our ends, et cetera."

"Ha ha."

Advertisements for discos were everywhere. Some offered air-conditioning, some beauty contests, one a Friday night watermelon-eating contest. Lots of posters for the Disco Romantika. Still we did not go, but walked along the beach after dinner or sipped ouzo outside at the small taverna we had discovered that first rainy evening. Two very talented men sang songs in Greek. Sometimes one or another of the young waiters from the Bungalows joined us.

"You go to disco?" they asked. "You no like?"

And so one night we get up our courage and do it.

"We don't have to stay," we assured one another as we remembered to take the flashlight, the key, some money.

"We can just look in, have an ouzo; no need to actually *hang around* if we don't like it." As we walk up the hill, I think how beautiful she is, my daughter, and how tonight her hair is exactly the same colour as the waxing moon.

The moon draws us — Come Come Come Come ("Travel the world and the Seven Seas / Everybody's lookin' for something") and we go in under the arch and the comical neon sign — *Disco Pomantika* — up the stairs to the balcony above the dance floor. Where the bar is. Where we will be able to observe all the goings-on. We sit down at a small wrought-iron table with a glass top.

What is probably tacky and gimcrack by day — the silly little tables, wrought iron painted white, with all their rococo decorations, the fountains and the fairy lights — is utterly magical on this summer night. It is early yet, by Greek standards, only about ten-thirty. Not very many people are dancing. Two little girls in white dresses, the older teaching the younger to do some steps, are having a grand time moving in and out of the circles of light. We order ouzo and water. The song changes to "Last Night a D.J. Saved My Life" and my daughter says rather wistfully that she would like to dance but doesn't like going to a place like this without a partner. Immediately, a partner appears, a tall thin waiter who has sat with us several times at the little taverna and is a very serious young man. He is thinking of joining the Communist Party; he believes there would be a more equal distribution of wealth if the Communists were in power. Whenever we ask him what a song means he always replies, "Is a very sad song."

"Are all the songs sad in Greece?" I ask him.

"Oh yes, all." Then he adds, "Are no happy mans in Greece, only happy childrens."

I sit up above the dance floor sipping my ouzo,

watching the people — there are more and more dancers on the floor now — wanting to dance myself but not sure who would ask me. When my daughter comes back from dancing with the tall thin waiter, she sits watching the dancers with a critical eye and suddenly says, "That couple are at the Bungalows. How old do you think they are?" She is talking about a very thin blond couple who are dancing up a storm in the middle of the floor. We've seen them on the beach and coming in and out of the dining-room with a little blond boy of about seven. The man wears mirror-faced sunglasses all the time, even at meals, and he is wearing them tonight, as well as tight red and black striped pants and a black T-shirt. She is wearing a Mickey Mouse T-shirt and a blue mini-skirt.

"I think they are about thirty-two," I say.

My daughter suggests that they are having a "last fling at youth." I tell her I will remind her of that remark when she is thirty-two.

The young Greek waiters from the resort hover around our table like bees. My daughter frowns, chooses one and descends once more to the marble dance floor. The man who has served us drinks and seems to be the general bartender/waiter for the whole establishment stops to ask if I want anything.

"Where you from?" He leans on the rail and looks down at my daughter, dancing.

"Canada."

A big smile. "Where Canada?"

"You mean where *is* it or where *in* Canada?"

"Where in? What city?"

"Vancouver."

Another big smile.

"I been. Four times. On boats."

When my daughter comes back this time we introduce ourselves.

"Don't you ever get time off to dance?" I say. It seems to me that he has looked longingly at the dancers.

"Too busy. Later." Then he looks straight at my daughter. "You dance me? Later?"

"Sure," she says.

"We aren't staying long," I remind her.

"Oh, right."

I want to dance. It's horrible music, pushy, insistent urban music which has nothing to do with this island, its history and culture. And the words to many of the songs are nasty; they don't bear thinking about. And yet. I could go down and dance by myself. I like to dance but I have the most horrible feeling that my daughter would not like it, that it would embarrass her to see her mother out there alone on the dance floor. There are a few people over thirty here but they are parts of families. A pretty French mother is dancing with her young son; the father dances with the baby sister, who keeps trying to catch the circles of light. I begin to feel like a chaperone or more accurately one of those Spanish duennas who followed well-bred Spanish girls around. All I need is a large mantilla, some jewels on my arthritic fingers, and an aristocratic nose.

The bartender comes by again and sets down two glasses of ouzo.

"I give," he says.

"Oh no, no thank you."

"You no like? What you want?"

"No no, I like. I like very much. But ouzo very

strong. Too much ouzo and — " I open my hands, let them fall on the table.

He nods, serious.

"Yes, very strong. I like dance to your daughter. Later."

I look up at him.

"How old are you?"

"How old you think?"

He is older than the young waiters but not much older.

"Twenty-four."

He smiles and nods.

"My daughter," I say, very carefully, in my best duenna manner, "is fifteen." I sit up a bit straighter, raise my chin, pull my mantilla a little tighter around my head.

We look at one another. "I good man," he says and I believe him.

She does not dance with him that night or the next, but on the third night he dances with her and she decides that even though he is as serious as the tall thin waiter (who is "too serious" in her eyes, too self-righteous) and his English is not so good as the crew-cut waiter who is studying business administration in Austin, Texas, she likes him. We are late coming to the disco that night because we have taken a bus trip to a place called Aliki Beach, where we swam and ate grilled fish and walked around the remains of a palace built by an ancient queen, a palace built to honour Eros. She also kept a harem of young boys and I can't help wondering at what age she took up this interesting hobby.

After the third night my daughter doesn't really dance with anyone else. He introduces us to his friends when they come to the disco. We smile and exchange greetings. Sometimes they send over drinks. I still want to dance but have accepted that this is not the right time or place to do so. And so I sip my ouzo and observe, while the dancers fling out their limbs in all directions and the yellow moon moves slowly across the sky like a snail in a golden shell.

And tonight she has gone up there alone, with my permission. Mikhalis, that is his name, has promised to walk her home after he finishes his work. And anyway, if one is on the shelf one might as well be there, not half on, half off. I worry a bit. I brought her on this trip to learn about Greece. Is Donna Summers Greece? Michael Jackson? The Disco Romantika? No more Greece than Bungalows Limenos. ("Travel the world and the Seven Seas / Everybody's lookin' for something / Sweet dreams are made of this.") But let me tell you a story.

Five-and-a-half years ago I spent a winter in Athens. In the pension where I was staying there was an Australian woman of about fifty, a wonderful woman, very handsome, very intelligent, who had a knack, no, more than that, a gift, for travelling around the world and meeting new and interesting people. It was her great desire that winter to learn some of the Greek dances, the old ones, and so she joined an organization called The Lyceum of Greek Women. As far as I could figure out, this was a cross between the Junior League and an historical society, and one of the things they did was to teach the old dances or hire teachers to do so, and to sponsor performances every Thursday night at a theatre in the centre of the city. I didn't join the dance classes because I was already, two days a week, struggling in the labyrinth of the Greek language as well as trying to finish a novel. But my friend Beryl joined and she enjoyed it very much.

In April The Lyceum of Greek Women had their annual dinner dance and Beryl was urged to come and bring some guests. It was to be a gala affair, at the George V Hotel, and she invited me and an Australian couple who were also staying at our pension. It was a strange evening. Heavily corseted ladies in dresses that seemed to come from another era (what my mother would have called "dinner dresses" in the forties) and in elaborate hairdos, hair often bleached blonde or dyed with henna — the same women one sees at Zonars or Floca on a winter afternoon, spooning up hot chocolate and gossiping with one another, biting into pastries, licking the cream from the edges of their mouths. These women had dragged along reluctant husbands in elegant business suits, gold cuff-links showing just at the edges of jacket sleeves, boredom showing too as they tapped cigarettes on the lids of their gold cigarette cases.

There was an emcee, a young Greek comedian-singer in a sequinned dinner jacket. He told jokes in Greek and kept tripping over his microphone cable. There was a band which played foxtrots, tangos and two-steps, and these well-to-do ladies and gentlemen pushed each other around the ballroom in a desultory fashion. And then, towards midnight, the band suddenly played the first few notes of what has become the Greek national dance, the "syrtaki," and the room fell silent.

Da da / da dah / dadadada dah. You know it. Anthony Quinn made it famous in *Zorba the Greek*. The women got up first. A few joined hands and began to dance, then more, then more. They laughed and their eyes shone like the eyes of young girls. They called to the men Come! Come! At first the men resisted, looked away, drummed on the table with their fingertips, lit another cigarette.

But their feet wouldn't stay still; their feet betrayed them. Under the tables their feet in those elegant leather shoes began to trace out the old steps and soon the men too were up and dancing, joining the ever-increasing line. A group of women rushed over to our table. Come! Come! Beryl was all right, of course, but I protested I didn't know how. "Doesn't matter!" they cried, "Doesn't matter!" and it didn't. I joined the dance as the music whirled us faster and faster and the George V ballroom became an enormous village square.

I've never forgotten it. I've never forgotten the feet of those men, the feet that would deny gold and silk and the years that stood between Athens and the country festivals these people had enjoyed when they were young. And the same thing will happen tonight at the Disco Romantika. At about two o'clock (we've stayed late, we've seen it happen) Mikhalis will shut off the tape loop and put on a record of the old dances. He knows them; all the young people know them. That is the amazing thing. "Come," they will say to my daughter, "come come come come come." And with her arms around the shoulders of strangers who have suddenly become friends, she too will join the dance.

Degrees

Degrees

She wasn't one of us. No amount of silver tea services or lace tablecloths or children's teas could make her so. And she didn't seem to know that, kept trying and trying until she was worn out, until when I looked at her one day, I thought: "That poor woman is at the end of her tether," and could really see it, her tether, see her straining to break away from it, but the rope only getting tighter and tighter until…Until. And I thought back to the remark she made to no one in particular, to the air or the merciless blue sky, a curious remark as she stepped down from the last of the rickety steps which had been pushed up against the airplane, stepped down and onto the red earth, which was one of the amazing things about that country, something I never got over, that earth the colour of flower pots or in some places darker, the colour of dried blood.

"Well," she said, blinking behind her spectacles, "well, this time we're determined to make a go of it."

I wasn't there, of course. It was Mary Lamb and

Norman and Mr Adonkóor, the Assistant Registrar, who stepped forward from under the shade of the airport roof and out into the midday sun. We hadn't arrived yet, and when we did it was by boat and then mini-bus up from the coast, and there was no official welcome, just an informal visit from Norman and Mary while Joseph, our cook-steward, was helping us string up musty mosquito nets, and the children were out in the garden staring with equal amazement at the lemon tree with its green lemons and the long stick carried by the night watchman. "To catch tief-man," he had told them, a phrase that none of us — then — understood.

Mary had brought a thermos of tea and some crumble tart and their dear little baby girl, and it was all very informal and cheerful. I was pregnant and not feeling too well, so Norman said he'd see the powers-that-be about getting us into a house on the compound as quickly as possible, and we appreciated all the kindness and the tips and the offer to come and pick us up once a day until we managed to buy a car. This was the beginning of the second year of their tour and they were old hands. Jason, my husband, asked about the other members of the department; and so we hadn't been in the country a full day when we heard about that curious chap, Roland Garwood, and his even more curious wife, Ruth. Mary repeated the remark she had heard or overheard, she wasn't sure which, as Ruth had been blinking against the glare and didn't seem to be looking at Mary, although she may have been or maybe would have been if she hadn't been blinking and squinting against the sun.

"It was such an extraordinary remark," Mary said. "And they've decided not to even try and get a house on the compound but to live off."

"As though they had something to hide," I said, and was sorry.

"Well, yes, but they're not antisocial; at least Ruth isn't. Roland doesn't say much, one way or the other. But we hadn't been in the car five minutes before Ruth was telling me about the yards and yards of muslin she'd shipped out to make curtains and her silver tea service and all the wonderful parties she plans to give for Dear Trevor."

"Dear Trevor?"

"Their little boy. He's adopted."

"Ruth is East Indian," Norman said.

"And Roland?"

"British. She's a nurse, so perhaps they met during the War. They aren't young, either of them. He's easily old enough to have been in the War."

"Is the child Indian or British?"

"Oh, completely Anglo-Saxon. Blond, blond curls and blue eyes and eyelashes girls would kill to have."

"He's a strange little chappie," Norman said. Norman was a nice, fresh-faced, rather pompous young Englishman in his late twenties, fond of phrases like "the powers-that-be." I stared at his long, pale legs. On the boat all the Englishmen had switched to shorts once we got round the Bay of Biscay, but I still found it a little amazing to see grown men dressed like Boy Scouts all day long.

"Anyway," Mary said, "you'll meet them soon enough. They had a car shipped out, and Ruth is a great one for dropping in."

"Does Roland come with her?"

"Oh yes, although she's going to hire a driver, she says. Roland comes with her and sits in a chair and smiles a strange smile, but hardly every says a word except about work."

"And the child? Does the child come too?"

"Oh yes. Trevor doesn't say much either. Just sucks his thumb and looks out at us all with his gorgeous blue eyes. I get the feeling that he doesn't really know how to play."

They went soon afterwards, these nice helpful people. They had explained to us the differences (not many) of shopping at the Kingsway or the UTC in town, had said we would need a washerman, and, when told what we intended to pay Joseph — the equivalent of forty-five dollars a month — looked at each other, and then Norman cleared his throat and smiled and said that was an awfully high wage for these parts, and don't let these chaps take advantage of you. We were forgiven, however, when we pointed out that Joseph's previous employer had paid only five shillings less, so it seemed reasonable to offer the same or a little better.

"You'll have to come to our Coffee Mornings," Mary said as they were leaving. "A group of us take turns, every Thursday."

"Drink coffee and outdo themselves trying to make the best cakes. Regular chin-wag. You know the sort of thing." Norman smiled a manly sort of smile at Jason as if to say, oh yes, we know these women.

I put it down then to all the fatigue and novelty and confusion, but I had a sudden intense and totally unwarranted dislike of Norman Lamb and his pretty, efficient wife. They had summed us up, nice serious husband, nice wife who was feeling a bit under the weather due to pregnancy, two pretty and polite daughters. I thought of the form-board puzzles that our younger daughter liked so much when she was even a toddler. Some of them were simply brightly coloured shapes which the baby had to turn around or "recognize" in such a way that she could fit them into the appropriate space on the form board. Purple triangles, orange squares, green parallelograms. There was one with people too, and cars, and railway trains. Mary and Norman had picked us up and, without much turning, had fitted us into the correct space. Or so they thought. Smug. That was the word. Norman particularly. Smug. Or "know-all" as Jason, born and brought up in England, might have put it.

As I fell asleep under the mended and musty mosquito net, all kinds of images came to mind. The mustiness reminded me of the first night at my grandfather's summer place when I was a child. The nets themselves, none too clean, a kind of grey-white, were like moths' wings in the summer dusk. The girls had gone right to sleep after supper, and Joseph had gone to his quarters next door. The broad, comforting back of my husband moved gently up and down beside me. I was the only person still awake, except, I supposed, the night watchman. The baby gave a little flutter inside me. I wondered if it would be affected by having been conceived in one climate and born in another. Presumably the climate inside me was fairly constant.

I thought again about Ruth Garwood. "Well, we're determined to make a go of it this time." What had happened last time? She was obviously someone who did not fit into the Lambs' orderly form board. But wanted to. Oh yes. Somehow I understood that right from the beginning. Understood well, not only from the tone of voice used by the Lambs, but because I, too, was not really "one of us" or only partially so, by virtue of being married to "one of us" and producing nice, well-mannered, good-looking children. But I wasn't

English, I was American — not the same thing at all; and I knew from personal and painful experience the enormous capacity the English had for rudeness to those they found different or inferior or maybe just plain threatening.

When we were first married we lived with Jason's parents and I was forever being called "you Americans" and doing the wrong thing. I would cook the cake at the wrong Regulo, so that it was hard as a rock and had to be served with custard; or bring back the wrong apples from the greengrocer's in the village. "Oh," she would say, peering into the basket. "Oh dear."

"What's the matter?"

(Laughs.) "Oh. Well. I thought I asked for cooking apples."

"Aren't these cooking apples?"

"Oh no, these are Granny Smiths. Terribly dear. The very best eating apples."

"I'll go back," I said. (All green apples were cooking apples where I grew up, so I'd just reached for them without asking for help.)

"Oh no. That long walk." (Sigh.) "Well, Father adores them. We can have a tin of apricots for sweet."

That sort of thing. The constant feeling that I should have known how to do these things, that I was not only different but inferior. Jason didn't make me feel that way, or seldom; somehow he had escaped from that awful insularity and had a truly adventurous spirit. He tended to fit in wherever he was, and to accept the otherness of other countries, other peoples. Which is why he had never regretted our move to Canada. Which was why, when the letter came from his old tutor (who was out in Africa and just about to leave:

would Jason be interested in taking over for a while?),
he was excited by the prospect even before he finished
the letter or knew, really — for the country had changed
its name since our schooldays — where we were being
asked to go to.

His father and uncles, on the other hand, called just
about everyone from Calais eastward "wogs" and spent
hours discussing how the Pakistanis were ruining
England. They all went abroad, of course, and had a
wonderful time, so long as they stayed together and
could order English breakfasts.

"Lucky you," said my mother-in-law, when we stopped
for a visit en route. "Fancy having servants."

In my mental wanderings, before I finally fell asleep
that first night, I imagined Ruth Garwood as a small
dark handsome woman in a bright sari, perhaps with a
caste mark in the middle of her forehead, my
stereotype picture of an Indian woman. In London and
Birmingham these women would be covered up with
overcoats and scarves, although their saris or trousers
would show underneath. Out here, in the tropics, such
encumbrances would not be necessary and all the
beauty and practicality of that beautiful form of dress
would be revealed. But I never saw Ruth in a sari,
not once, although the Dean's wife and the Vice-
Chancellor's wife and many African women always
wore their native dress and really dressed up for official
functions. But that was all right — for them. They were
proud of being African; they had power and were just
beginning to glory in it. Ruth was not proud of being
Indian; she wanted to be English. And she was in-
credibly plain, almost ugly, with none of the innate
handsomeness of most Indian women I'd seen. Her
skin was a pale yellow-brown and she had several black

moles on her cheeks. She wore the kind of dresses that used to be called "housedresses" when I was growing up, not things you actually wore out on the street, but dresses bought because they were cotton and cheap and washed well. We all wore cotton, of course, and I, a clumsy sewer at best, had spent hours making pretty sleeveless frocks for my little daughters and sleeveless frocks for myself. I intended to make more, from the wax prints and famous indigo tie-dye cloth, as soon as I knew my way around the market and had some idea of prices. Mary Lamb's dress that first night had been extremely simple but was very stylish; Ruth, at first and then at subsequent meetings, always looked as though she were dressed in the kind of awful dresses one finds in the very cheapest department stores or bargain basements. She wore gold-rimmed spectacles and I think her eyes were extremely sensitive to light, for she was always blinking. And her voice! Well, all I can think of is the Queen's Christmas message, which we still sometimes listen to (and imitate) just for fun. Every word was perfectly enunciated. It was elocution English: it was totally unreal. Ruth did not really talk, she declaimed. At one of the few Coffee Mornings that I ever went to, someone who was being kind had brought Ruth along (she was never actually asked, she was never part of the group). It was a terribly hot day, and yet that week's hostess had knocked herself out making maid-of-honour tarts and jam sponge in a kitchen that must have been over one hundred degrees. "The Heat" (we were at the end of the Rainy Season and moving into the Dry Season and the parching, red dust-fog of the Harmattan would soon begin) was one of the main topics of conversation, along with the usual gossip about babies and pregnancies and how tiresome the servants were and the shortages. Someone asked Ruth about Trevor, who was too young for the University Nursery School and lived off the compound, so we didn't see him as often as most of the other children.

"Dear Trevor is suffering terribly from the heat; he's so fair, you know." She took a sip of her tea (she never touched coffee, thank you) and added, in that incredible colonial voice, "And I, too, am suffering from the heat. It is very difficult."

She must have seen or sensed some of the women exchanging glances (how could an Indian woman suffer from the heat?), for she added, very firmly, "Oh yes, I am not used to this. We always spent our summers in the mountains."

This became a kind of awful in-joke with the women. "How are you standing the heat?" "Oh, I'm suffering terribly, my Dear. You know we always spent our summers in the moun-taynes." Then the women would giggle like small girls. Oh, aren't we naughty?

One woman, whose parents had been out in India during the last days of the Raj, wondered openly what "Daddy" had done in the Civil or Military that allowed him and his family the privilege of fleeing to the hill stations when the hot weather came. But nobody bothered to ask. These women, who were so curious about every tiny detail of each other's lives, really didn't care about Ruth's past, or only in a desultory fashion. She wasn't interesting because she didn't count.

Some time towards the end of the first month of our "tour" we were invited to Sunday lunch at the Garwoods'. Most servants had Sunday off, at least from after breakfast until Monday morning, but not Ruth's.

I'm not sure when they did get time off, but their way to retaliate was simply to quit. The first couple of times, she refused to sign their book (and without her signature they would have trouble getting another job, especially with the University people, who did not beat them or berate them as did their native masters and mistresses), but they threatened to report her to the Vice-Chancellor for overworking and underpaying them, and somehow the threat worked. However, she chose to say that she had "dismissed" them and then would add, in that awful voice, "One just can't get good servants these days." And sigh. And so Samuel would be replaced by Kobena, who would be replaced by Enoch, and so on. Joseph, our steward, would tell me gossip about her, leaning on his broom and laughing.

"That woman, Madame, that Missus Garwood, she's a bad woman, Madame." I knew I shouldn't encourage him, that I would be indulging in the kind of gossip I openly detested. But he knew I would ask.

"Why, Joseph? Why is she bad?"

He would laugh and shake his head and give a couple of token sweeps to the floor. "Big trouble, Madame. She is no good at-tall!"

Then he would laugh and shake his head and go back to work. So the servants gossiped about her, too. Poor woman, I thought, poor woman.

But she asked for it. She did not like Africans and she made that very clear. A lot of English didn't like Africans either, particularly a lot of the English women; but they were white and somehow got away with it, probably because there were too many generations of whites giving orders for the servant class to see anything unusual about imperious tones coming forth from a white face. Indeed Joseph, who had had some education at mission schools, often harkened back to "Gold Coast time," especially if we were giving a dinner party. He would survey the side dishes for the curry (toasted and plain coconut, chopped pawpaw, bananas, roasted ground nuts, chopped egg, and so on), count them up on his fingers, and then shake his head sadly.

"In Gold Coast time, Madame, twenty-one side dishes. Minimal, Madame, min-i-mal." He loved to cook and longed for the good old days of colonial extravagance.

As did Ruth, only for different reasons. That first visit, I had some glimpse of why Joseph called Ruth a "bad woman." It was very hot, as usual, and yet the table was laid for an elaborate meal, which I suspect that none of us really wanted. There was a huge roast of pork from pig bought at the University's model farm. Ruth wouldn't buy meat at the public market because it was so disgusting there, my Dear. She got chickens and eggs up towards the Catholic school and pig from the farm and whatever else she needed in the way of meat from Sam's Cold Store in town. But she was not alone in this, and I admit that when I wanted meat from the market, or a chicken, I used the excuse of my pregnancy and the heat and the cheaper prices if an African were buying, and sent Joseph off to haggle and bargain and deal with the flies and the smell. There were roast potatoes instead of yams, and creamed onions, and sherry trifle for desert. There was no wine — it was almost impossible to get hold of wine unless one was with an American firm or with the UN — but there was imported beer instead of Star or Club, and fresh lemonade for the children. The table glittered with crystal and silver.

We began with a fruit cocktail and when everyone was finished but Dear Trevor — who, when we arrived, had been riding his tricycle round and round the veranda and hadn't wanted to come to lunch at all — Ruth picked up a little bell and rang it. Rang it imperiously. Shook it hard. There was nothing soft or discreet about this bell; it had the same tone as those breast-shaped bells one finds in stores where the proprietor might be eating his lunch at the back. There is usually a little sign underneath: "Ring bell for service." She smiled at us.

"Mummy's bell," she said.

"Oh God," Roland said, and let out a large guffaw, and then a belch. I realized he was terribly drunk, although he had seemed quite sober when he greeted us. He already had a reputation at the Staff Club. Norman Lamb pink-faced and smiling, shaking his head but loving the naughtiness of it (Norman who exposed his long pale legs but always kept his feet well covered up), said he even had a mistress on one of the narrower streets in town.

Nothing happened. The three-bladed fan circled lazily over our heads. Dear Trevor sat with his thumb in his mouth, watching his mother. She rang the bell again, this time calling out in a loud voice, "Boy, Boy!"

"Kofi," Roland said, "his name is Kofi."

"Oh yes, of course. I never can remember. Would you mind going to see what's holding things up?"

"You go," he said. "It's your bloody party."

"Perhaps he has a radio on," Jason suggested. "Can't hear the bell."

I wondered, but not aloud, if he had simply downed tools and quit.

Ruth excused herself and went out to the kitchen. I

don't know exactly what she found there, or what she said, but she returned very quickly with an absolutely piratical-looking man, an enormous man with a long tribal mark across one cheek. He wore the usual faded khaki shorts and white mess jacket, standard dress for serving at a small lunch or dinner party. Ruth went around the table with a brass tray, clearing away the fruit cocktail dishes, and the cook-steward slammed down the platter with the joint in front of Roland. Then he shuffled back to the kitchen for the veg and we all stared in embarrassment at the platter. Great hunks of meat had been whacked off any which way and it was obvious, from the shining lips of the steward, what he had been up to when Ruth rang her bell.

Roland guffawed again. "Serves you right, my Dear, for making that poor bugger work on a Sunday."

The potatoes were hard at the centre and the gravy full of lumps. Nobody ate much, but both Roland and Jason drank quite a lot of beer. Our two daughters, who were usually quite talkative and lively and loved to go visiting, were stunned into silence by the tension in the room. When Christa, our youngest, asked Trevor if she could ride his tricycle, he said no; and when Ruth said, "Manners, darling, manners," he screamed, "No!" and jumped off his chair. I was surprised to see Roland, who had been getting such detached and sardonic amusement out of the whole fiasco, come to the rescue by inviting both girls out onto the veranda and then producing all kinds of wonderful trucks and trains and things with propellers that he had obviously made himself. He knelt down with them and played and I saw him once or twice put his hand very gently on the golden head of his son. It was clear then that he loved the little boy very much.

We sat inside, with the door open, drinking tea and listening to Ruth ramble on about the Lebanese family who actually owned this house and lived in the downstairs half. A very important man, very charming, with such a charming wife and sweetly pretty daughters. The Africans did not like the Lebanese because so many of them were merchants who made a lot of money and sent it all out of the country. There were rumours that the government was going to crack down, perhaps expel them from the country or not allow them to own a business. The English didn't like the Lebanese either — real wogs, don't you know, not to be trusted — although the women on the compound often went to Baboo Bazaar or similar dry-goods stores when they wanted more material for the dresses they were always "running up." (It amused me how these women were always "running up" something or "dashing off" a letter or "dashing" to town or "popping in." I suppose it gave their lives an illusion of urgency and importance they might otherwise have lacked.) Ruth would have to learn to dislike the Lebanese if she really wanted to be English.

And then she switched to a story about how she had "dealt" with a drunken African who had been yelling and singing under their windows earlier in the week.

"So I went down," she said, "and I walked right up to him and said, 'I want you to know what my little boy said to me just now. He said, Mummy, is there an animal outside? And I said, No, my pet, it's just a poor drunken man who doesn't know he's frightening my little boy. And he said, Mummy, I think there's an animal down there. So I told my little boy, Mummy will go down and tell the poor man he's frightening you. And the poor mite screamed and held onto me and thought I would surely be eaten up by this animal he could hear howling and crying out down below his window.'" On and on and on. In the car I told Jason I never wanted to go there again, that I would plead my pregnancy and she, being a nurse, would understand without being hurt.

And I kept my word, right up to the time of Dear Trevor's third birthday party. I didn't go much of anywhere, for my legs had swelled and there was some anxiety about the baby. So I sat on the veranda, with my feet propped up on a chair, and read, or dozed or talked to Joseph, who had become my compound "newspaper," or wondered, in a lazy manner, about all the factions and hierarchies there were at this place; it was more complicated and subtle than the hierarchies of angels in the Bible.

Some of the women, especially the Department wives, regularly "popped in" to see how I was getting along, or ask if there were something special I wanted in town. They continued to give me all sorts of advice — that next year I must take my children out of the University Primary School and Nursery School and put them into the private school, I think it was called "The Hill," but I don't really remember now. Much smaller classes — fewer Africans, they meant — and much higher standards. Mary Lamb told me poor old Ruth was on her tenth steward and recounted an experience horribly similar to ours, except that the cook, when he didn't answer the bell, was discovered kicking slices of turkey under the table. She imitated Ruth, knocking on the door of the manager of the UTC (the second-largest supermarket/trading company in town) and saying how her little boy must have some butter, real butter — that he could not, would not eat anything else!

And Dear Trevor, with his wonderful golden curls and long eyelashes, sucking his thumb, would be exhibited, and somehow a brown-wrapped parcel of the precious rationed butter would exchange hands.

But we all did that; we all knocked on the door of the manager of the Kingsway or the UTC and asked if there were any butter in this week. We didn't always get it (and the tinned butter, when it was available, had a horrid, rancid taste). Ruth almost invariably did. I expect she gave a "dash," or bribe, a perfectly acceptable way of doing business in that country. But we English ladies would never stoop to that, however much we did want a little bit of butter for our bread. Mary Lamb came by on Sundays and took our children to Sunday school, and when they came home they sang to us about the Foolish Man Who Built His House Upon The Sand/

And the Rain/
Came/
Tum-/
Bling/
Down.

Ruth came to visit too. She'd got her driver's licence and would drive up to the University around tea-time (she had finally got Dear Trevor into the private nursery school) and "pop in." Joseph hated her. She would go out in the kitchen and inspect it for cleanliness, and tell me in a loud voice that I should keep my fridge locked AT ALL TIMES, you couldn't be too careful. I didn't like her doing this and kept meaning to tell her off, but I was too lethargic — or cowardly — to do it. And she always had that bright, determined smile on her face, that smile that said you see, this time we're going to make a go of it.

Jason said that Roland was a brilliant teacher and
that all his students loved him. But I hardly ever saw
him, unless Jason came back during the eleven-o'clock
break and took me for coffee at the Club. Roland would
smile at me wickedly and ask when I was going to come
up and see his epidiascope.

Christmas came and went. It didn't seem much like
Christmas, it was so hot. The Senior Staff Club gave a
children's party and a Junior Staff member played
Father Christmas in a red suit and white mask. His
brown hands looked very strange, and Trevor cried and
cried and refused to go up and get his gift. This set off
a lot of the other children, including Christa, and was
very embarrassing for everybody; but Ruth just smiled
and blinked and stared straight ahead.

The invitation to Trevor's birthday party ("Daddies
and Mummies invited too") came in mid-January. I was
almost seven months pregnant, very heavy and dreamy,
so thankful for Joseph and Jason and the fact that I
could vegetate ninety percent of the time. I was longing
for rain, but they told me my baby would most likely be
born before the rains began again. I told Jason I didn't
want to go to the party. He looked uncomfortable.

"Look here," he said, "you don't have to go, of course.
I can take Jennifer and Christa. But Roland particularly
asked me if you'd be able to come."

"Roland did!"

"Yes. He thinks maybe Ruth is really crazy, he's not
sure. He's trying to persuade her to see somebody. And
he says that he doesn't really blame the women because
Ruth is impossible, but that they are being horribly
cruel. They don't ask her to the Coffee Mornings…"

"Lucky her!"

"Yes, you may feel that way, but she wants to go,

she's desperate to go. She told one of the women she'd be delighted to have a Coffee Morning at her house, and the woman said oh well, they'd more or less arranged it for the next few months and anyway, it was sort of a tradition to have them on the compound. Or sometimes she'll arrive someplace and actually hear the woman call to the steward and say, 'Tell her I'm not home.' Roland says she minds even more for Trevor than she does for herself; he often isn't invited to the children's parties because she'd have to be invited too."

"But what can I do? I don't like her either. I may understand her, or partly, but I don't really like her. She wants to be the worst sort of Englishwoman, and God knows there's enough of those around."

"I think Roland's afraid that nobody will come and that Ruth will go right off the deep end."

"They wouldn't be that mean."

"They might be."

"Well, what can I do?"

"Perhaps if you wrote little notes…"

"Little notes?"

"Yes."

"Jason," I said, "I'm not one of them either; you know that. I don't have that kind of power." I sighed. "But I know someone who does. Ask Joseph if he'll stay on for an hour tonight, and then I just have to make one call."

"The Lambs?"

"Where else?"

I felt cross and resentful, as if all of a sudden I were caught in some awful double bind, which left me, whichever way I turned, playing for the wrong team. But I knew Mary Lamb could fix it, at least so far as the party went. She was liked by everyone, the right sort of woman who did all her own baking and yet managed to always look cool and sweet, who had brought out not silly things like silver tea services and crystal but extra pairs of sandals in graduated sizes so little Diana wouldn't be reduced to wearing market sandals or plastic sandals like the children of the Russian and Polish lecturers. Brought out birthday candles and party favours and knicker elastic — practical, useful things. She and Norman were sitting in the lounge of their pretty bungalow, drinking tea and looking at travel brochures — they were planning to go to the Canary Islands before they went home on leave. They looked up, surprised to see us, me particularly; and because they really were nice people, they immediately got up and came forward to greet us, saying they hoped there wasn't anything wrong.

If If If. If I had refused to go to bat for Ruth. If I could have persuaded Roland to persuade Ruth to call off the party. But why, how? It was Trevor's birthday, after all. He was entitled to a party. Children's parties were a very large part of the social life out there. And even if Trevor had simply been with his mother and father, the same thing could have happened. What was so awful, what kept us all shocked and stunned for days, was the fact that it could have happened to any of us — that it was a tragedy that had, in the end, nothing to do with the sad affair of Ruth and Roland and their unhappy marriage.

Everyone who had been invited came. Of course. Mary Lamb saw to that. I could imagine her making the rounds, being pleasant but firm, putting the emphasis on Trevor, on the fact that it was his birthday, poor little chappie, no reason why he should have to suffer.

We were late getting there, and the large lounge and
even the veranda were filled to overflowing with little
boys in smart khaki shorts and gleaming white shirts,
little girls in cotton party dresses. Each of the boys was
given a packet of Plasticine and each of the girls a
bright new hair ribbon. Roland organized the games,
while the rest of us sipped long drinks and smiled at all
the pretty children. Except for the two rather plump
Lebanese girls from downstairs (in very elaborate nylon
party dresses and covered with gold bracelets, earrings,
necklaces), all of the children were white. Although
there were several Africans in our Department, and one
with an Irish wife, none of these people had been invited. Ruth, amongst all this Britishness, looked more
yellow and wizened and out of place than ever. She had
on a silk dress, in honour of the occasion, but it was in
the same dark blues and muddy browns as her usual
day dresses, and hung off her, really hung off her. She
couldn't have weighed more than eighty pounds. A long
table had been laid out at one side of the room and
there were jellies and cakes and sandwiches all neatly
protected by cheesecloth cloches. A few of the older
boys had already swiped the odd sandwich and Ruth
told them, with a high, forced laugh, that they wouldn't
have to wait much longer, darlings, tea would be served
right after the games.

Trevor didn't seem to be very interested in his
presents, but Ruth made him say a formal thank-you for
each one. There were a lot of fairy tale books, Russian
or Chinese, which were quite lovely and available at the
University bookstore; there were hankies, a puzzle, a
box of crayons. Nobody went in for elaborate gifts at
these parties; there were just too many of them. But the
girls from downstairs, who had been brought to the

party by their nurse-girl, presented Trevor with a gold
wristwatch. You could see the Mummies and Daddies
look at each other. So vulgar. So out of place. Roland's
gift to his son was a wonderful wild-eyed handmade
rocking horse that Trevor wouldn't let anyone else ride.
When one little girl pointed out that he had to give
turns, it was bad manners if he didn't, he gave her such
a kick it made her cry. Ruth told Trevor he was a very
naughty boy and if he didn't mind his manners there'd
be no more party for him and Trevor replied that he
didn't care.

I had thought Roland was cold sober, but when Trevor
told Ruth he didn't care about the rotten old party, his
father let out one of his awful guffaws and said, "Out of
the mouths of babes, my Dear. Are you going to explain
to the child that the party isn't really for him?" Ruth
smiled even more gaily and said wasn't he a dreadful
man, and gave the little girl who'd been kicked an
extra hair ribbon. I was sad that Roland, who had
wanted the party to be such a success that he had
actually confided in me, or in me via my husband,
could not have held his tongue. Trevor looked from
one to the other and then ran out onto the veranda
and began riding his tricycle round and round shouting,
"Vroom Vroom get out of my way, Vroom Vroom get out
of my way," until Roland went firmly across the room
with the intention of stopping him at the same time
as Trevor, probably realizing he had gone too far,
abandoned his tricycle and came running back in. They
collided and Trevor fell down on the terrazzo floor and
bumped his head.

"Did you see that?" Ruth cried wildly. "Did you see
how he deliberately tripped the child?"

"Oh shut up," Roland said. "I did nothing of the

sort," and Mary Lamb said loudly, "Do you think the children might have their tea?"

Roland nodded and went off, without asking, to fetch the steward and the small boy to help with the handing round. The sandwiches were very good, and there were bowls of roasted groundnuts and jellies in all kinds of wonderful shapes (a point for Ruth, I could see, for she must have brought out or ordered the moulds from England) and a really splendid birthday cake made by one of the caterers in town. It certainly could not be called a totally unsuccessful party. I did not look at Roland, however, avoided his gaze, for I felt that by his outburst he had really let me down. Trevor seemed to have recovered his equilibrium and was cramming food into his mouth, red-faced and giggling, just like any other normal little birthday boy. Once he choked and had to be patted on the back, but that was always happening at parties.

A week later he was dead. I didn't hear about it at first; I think Jason worried about the effect of the news on me and the baby. So it was Joseph who told me about the "big trouble" over at the Garwoods' place. "The little boy be dead, Madame."

"Dead. What d'you mean dead?"

"Dead proper, Madame. They take him to hospital but he die anyway."

"When, Joseph?"

"I don't know, Madame. Monday, Tuesday."

"What did he die from?"

Joseph shrugged. He did not know.

I was frantic. We had no telephone. Jason had the car and I knew I shouldn't walk anywhere in that heat; I'd had a few ominous pains in the night. I knew I could send Joseph round with a note to Mary Lamb's but I didn't want to, I simply did not want to hear it from her. I would have to wait. I would have to sit there and wait until Jason came home for lunch. First I wondered which one of them had killed him. Had he got in the way of a thrown knife or a broken bottle? Then I saw him riding round and round on the veranda on his tricycle, shouting vroom, vroom, get out of my way, going faster and faster and somehow going down the steep steps, still on his bike, smashing his head open as he fell. I even wondered if one of the former stewards had come back and killed him. Vengeance was still a strong motive out here. Joseph himself told me how he had had "medicine" put in his soup when he went to confront his wife's lover. He was in hospital for a long time. "Sick proper."

Jason told me as soon as the children went off for their afternoon nap. It was silly and bizarre and horrible. Trevor had inhaled a groundnut into his lung, the nut had festered, the lung collapsed, and the child died. They only found out what it was during the autopsy.

"But weren't there any symptoms?" I cried. "No indication that he'd inhaled a peanut?"

Apparently not. He'd had a cough when he went to bed, but they put it down to overexcitement. Two days later he was unconscious. Both Roland and Ruth were sure it was some awful concussion from that tumble he took.

"Would they have been able to save him if they'd known what it was?"

"There's something called a bronchioscope, but it turns out the hospital in town didn't have one. So no, not here. They couldn't have saved him here. In the capital, yes, if they'd got him there in time."

That night, for the first time, I was afraid. What if something went wrong with me? What if something happened to Jennifer or Christa? To Jason? There were snakes out here, and rabid dogs, and fevers so numerous and mysterious they didn't even have names. What were we doing out here? Why had we come?

I didn't go to Trevor's funeral. Apparently Ruth had wanted to take the little boy home to England, but Roland had insisted he be buried out there, in the small English cemetery beyond the town. It seemed a strange thing to do, at the time. Ruth left a few days later and Roland moved into one of the flats behind Queen's Hall. God knows what happened to Ruth or all the silver and crystal and yards of muslin for curtains. I always feel very badly when I think that I made no effort to contact her other than a short note, which Jason took with him to the funeral. She didn't reply; I hadn't expected her to.

I understand that Roland is still out there.

I wonder if he stays because he wants to be close to his son. And I wonder what happened to all those handmade toys, especially the magnificent painted horse with the wild eyes. Roland did not keep a stiff upper lip at the funeral. He wept openly and even, so they said, at one point howled. It was Ruth who behaved in the proper manner and gained at the last, a little admiration and respect. It was Norman and Mary Lamb who went out to the airport to see her off.

Breaking the Ice

Breaking the Ice

The lines were down again. A voice on the radio was saying, "Is it ever too cold to snow? No, although it's sometimes too cold for snow to fall in fla..." then the lights went out and the radio went dead. A tree had blown over, no doubt — it happened at least once every winter, but didn't affect her much because she used a wood stove for cooking and heat, and had oil lamps and emergency candles as well as electric light.

It was just coming on dark when the electricity failed, so she lit the lamps and took a candle with her into the bathroom where her bath lay waiting. She always filled the tub with hot water and then let it cool down just enough to allow her to get in. In the chilly bathroom her body, when she rubbed it with the washcloth, gave off an aura of steam. The flame from the candle flickered and danced in the draft and cast enormous shadow-dancers on the walls. She stayed in the bath as long as she could — from now on until the lines were fixed, hot water meant heating kettles on the stove. It was Christmas Eve. Unless the hydro crew could find and fix the trouble tonight, there was a good chance the power would be out until the 27th at least. For who would want to go out on Christmas Day or even Boxing Day? Or maybe the hydro men wouldn't mind — if they got time-and-a-half or more and could become local heroes in the bargain. Sipping on a glass of sherry as she dried her hair in front of the pot-belly stove, Martha imagined all the pale, plump turkeys lying on kitchen counters, waiting to be stuffed tomorrow morning and popped into the oven. All the potatoes and yams; all the Brussels sprouts. And the Christmas lights. And the televisions. And the grandchildren, over for the holidays, who would want to pee or shit in the middle of the night. Even families who still had outhouses as well as flush toilets would find life very inconvenient; the snow was quite deep and it was cold out there, with the temperature falling. And one of the cardinal rules about outhouses was that they weren't built very close to the house. She was lucky; she even had an enormous chamber-pot as well as an outhouse. It was white enamel over metal and had a large flower, a red and blue chrysanthemum, stencilled on the bottom. The pot had been a humorous Christmas present several years ago but had turned out to be useful on cold winter nights when even going from warm bed to cold bathroom was an ordeal.

"So I'm all right, Jack," Martha said to her wavering reflection as she brushed her hair in front of the mirror in the children's room. The mirror was bad enough in ordinary light — it was old and the image wavered; by candlelight she saw a ghost or the face of a woman looking up at her from beneath several inches of water. As soon as she had decided to go to the Blandings' annual party, she had determined to really dress up, to wear a long wool skirt and a silk blouse, instead of her usual trousers and mended sweater. She would have to hold the skirt up above her boots to keep it from dragging in the snow, but it was important to look nice. A matter of pride. And make-up as well, so no one would know she'd been crying. The Blandings had their own generator, for emergencies such as this, so the party would definitely still be on. She imitated Mrs Blanding's voice, slightly nasal and with something perpetually negative about it, the sound equivalent of a turned-down mouth. "I suppose it's Peter's turn to have the children; that must be very hard on you." But she meant to be interested and kind then.

"Hard on me?" Martha said, smiling, baring her teeth at her reflection. "Oh no, it's only fair." Then she put down her brush in despair. Unbearable, that was all. She should be used to this by now; why didn't she get used to things? There was something neurotic about people who didn't get used to things, something not quite nice. It was embarrassing to be around such people. She was glad that she had come over to the island, at least; this was far better than being in the same city. And the telephone with its thick black umbilical cord, linking her, if she wished, to the outside world, the telephone was dead too. So she would be spared any phone calls from her children. "Merry Christmas, Mum. Are you all right over there?" "Perfectly all right." When what she really was was Perfectly All Wrong.

She had met her ex-husband in a coffee shop two days before, where she had given him the parcels for the girls: three boxes done up in brown paper, tied with red string and sealed with red sealing wax. DO

NOT OPEN BEFORE. Inside each box were lots of small presents — sugar mice, second-hand copies of *Little Women, Hans Brinker and the Silver Skates*, Gray's *Anatomy*, wind-up toys, puzzles, a wool sweater for each as their "real" present. Even a lump of coal in case they'd been bad. She loved buying presents and making them as well — jams and jellies, shortbreads, pot-pourri and hand-dipped candles. The whole family helped, or used to. Sometimes there had been house parties over here as well — everybody sleeping on the floor, drinking wine and playing silly games like Charades and Dictionary. Going for long walks. One year someone had brought an enormous jigsaw puzzle and everybody got fed up doing it so they threw it all over the house. She still, occasionally, found a section of barn or a piece of the sky that had worked its way up from some deep crevice or crack. "Autumn in New England."

In the shopping bag her ex-husband had given her was, among other things, a long, lumpy grey stocking, stapled shut, with a red bow and with a candy cane sticking out. Every time she looked at it now, she cried. How did you open a stocking by yourself?

"Well," her husband said, reaching for the bill.

"Well," she said.

"Take care of yourself." She watched him disappear down the street.

"No, it's not *hard*," Martha repeated to the imaginary Mrs Blanding.

But what a beautiful evening, and far better to walk up the road to a house full of merry people than to sit moping at the cottage, alone except for the old cat who still lived over here but was cared for by the couple at the store. So she built up the fire, put a hot-water bottle in the bed and set off carrying an old station lantern that she had found in a junkyard years ago. But when she got to the bottom of the path, the moonlight on the snow was so bright she decided to blow out the lantern; she didn't need it after all. It was partly for effect anyway — Martha arriving at the door of the party in her long wool cloak, carrying a lamp. She knew the way even if it had been pitch black. "The horse knows the way to carry the sleigh…"

In the moonlight the trees looked as though they were made of coral, and the whole landscape sparkled and shone. If it hadn't been so cold she could imagine she was in some strange, tropical country with dunes and beaches and houses covered in glittering white sand. Down below her and farther along towards the pass, the sea-lions, on their annual visit south, continued their amorous wrangle, roaring and barking. "She's mine; no, she's mine; no, she's mine." They sounded very eerie, especially in the dark, when you couldn't see them. Imagine someone visiting, someone who hadn't been told, waking up in the middle of the night to that? In this magical, glittering landscape one could conjure up real lions suddenly appearing from behind the trees, lions covered in white fur, soft as velvet, the males with enormous fur manes and crystal teeth. Lions covered in white fur and with bright blue eyes shining in the light of the moon.

The snow creaked under her heavy boots and she lifted up her cloak and her skirt so that they wouldn't get too wet. She carried a basket as well as the lantern. Her slippers were in the basket along with a few presents for the family. She began to hum a song she had known years ago, in another country, another time.

Over the river, and through the wood
To grandfather's house we go;
The horse knows the way
To carry the sleigh
Through the white and drifted snow, oh.

There had been one family still, in her town, who actually had a horse-drawn sleigh, a wonderful black thing,
a sleigh out of a fairy tale. The daughter of the family
was in Martha's class at school. How the little girls com-
peted to be "best friends" with this girl in the winter
time! Her mother, who was a fairy-tale illustration herself
in a severe but beautifully cut black coat and a black fur
hat, would very occasionally call for the child and allow
her to choose one friend to come back for cocoa and
cookies. Any one of them could have cocoa and cookies
at home, of course, but in no other case would they be
driven to cocoa and cookies in a black sleigh, wrapped
up in a tartan rug. For one entire winter Martha was the
favourite; she was never sure why. This girl also had a
horse of her own and a collie and an English nanny called "Awnie," who slept in the next bedroom.

Could there really have been enough snow on the
streets to be driven around in a sleigh? Perhaps it only
happened once or twice and her memory had performed a multiplication. It didn't matter — all that was
long ago. But wouldn't it be fun to have that sleigh
tonight, the sleigh and the chestnut horse and the
tartan rug and go riding from one end of the island
and back again, beneath a moon so white it looked as
though it were made of marble or thick ice? There
were horses on the island and no doubt someone had a
big wagon. Perhaps next year they could organize a hay-
ride, at least; you didn't even need snow for that.

Meanwhile, what about this year? How did you open a stocking by yourself?

Over the river and through the woods. But not a river here — the ocean, with the moonlight shining down on it, making it look like a wrinkled sheet of grey satin. Through the woods, however. She turned off the main road and now, with trees towering on either side of a narrow path, she stopped to light the lantern once more. The air smelled of wood-smoke and the sea. Up the path by the small wooden sign, "Blandings," hanging on a tree, then down, and there she was stamping her feet and laughing as Helen Blanding opened the door.

It was the usual gathering, mostly family. Sons and daughters, their wives and husbands, the grandchildren. Martha took off her boots, put on her slippers and offered her gifts. An enormous fir-tree dominated the living-room and Mr Blanding was helping the smallest grandchild tie an ornament to a low branch. The Blandings had just been to Mexico and had brought back wonderful ornaments of coloured tin, stars and angels and birds. Even an elephant. Martha imagined the workers in the ornament factory, cutting out this strange creature, the elephant. Still, no stranger than angels or five-pointed stars, although they of course saw those in the churches.

"The tree is lovely," she said. Then took a deep breath and waited for what she knew was coming.

"I suppose it's Peter's turn to have the children this Christmas. That must be very hard on you."

Just after midnight, one of the Blanding brothers walked her home. (Merry Christmas, Merry Christmas! Everyone had gathered at the door to call goodbye.)

"I don't like the thought of you going into that empty house," the brother said.

"That's just the trouble, it isn't empty; it's full of memories. And besides, the cat's there."

They stopped at the bottom of her path. The store had its generator working — puh-puh-puh-puh-puh-puh-puh — and had left its outside Christmas lights on all night.

"Silent Night," Martha said. "Except for the sound of generators and sea-lions. Oh well, it was no doubt very noisy in the manger. It even says so, right there in the carol — 'the cattle were lowing.' Lowing is just poetic for bellowing."

"And all the angels singing." They laughed. "Are you sure you won't have Christmas dinner with the mob?" he said. "It would be a favour to us, break up the family dynamic a bit. Everyone would be on their best behaviour."

"No — I'm just going to treat it like any other day. Besides, I get to listen to the 'Messiah' all the way through without interruption."

"If the power comes back on."

"Yes."

"If it's just like any other day, why not have dinner with us?"

She shook her head and went up the path. She knew he would wait at the bottom until he saw her light a lamp or candle. Nice person, she thought, as she put some more wood on the stove, nice people, the Blandings. Even the mother means well. One of the daughters had said, as they sat together on the sofa, sipping mulled wine, "Is there any romance looming?"

"You mean a 'significant other'? I heard someone actually use that term a few days ago. No, I don't think so. Or I don't know yet. Anyway, 'loom' is too large a word for it and sounds menacing. We'll see." She quickly changed the subject, not wanting to talk about it — him — not wanting to want. She got up and went to join the group singing carols around the portable organ.

> Oh the rising of the su·un
> And the running of the deer

The lights came on towards the end of the night, the radio as well, and she woke up startled and confused. The telephone was working too — "Merry Christmas, Merry Christmas." They forgot to ask how did you like your stocking, but she opened it anyway, sitting at the kitchen table. The children had obviously been to Chinatown: sandalwood soap, a pencil sharpener in the shape of a fat little Chinese boy sitting on a tomato, sparklers, a pretty fan. Also an enormous lollipop — "Redheads make better lovers," it said. She went outside to get wood, the old cat stepping high and dainty, shaking the snow from her paws, complaining.

"You don't have to be out here," Martha said. But perhaps the cat had missed her, in spite of all the spoiling from the couple at the store. They had tried her in the city; she was afraid to go outside and shat in all the corners. And so they brought her back and made an arrangement with the store.

There were bird-tracks everywhere and the prints of a raccoon. Martha lay down and made an angel in the snow. It didn't work too well because of the slight crust on top but it was definitely an angel. Or perhaps a bat? What was it about leaving one's mark in the snow? Probably the same urge, on a smaller scale, that prompted people to write their names on rocks or step in wet cement. "I was here." "Lo, I am with you always."

She made apple pie with a jar of apples they had put up in the autumn. The Blandings called — "Are you sure you won't?" She read; she listened to the radio, the cat curled up at the foot of the big bed. She was okay; it wasn't such an awful thing to be alone on Christmas Day, especially with the fires going well in the stoves, and a bottle of sherry, and a nice smell of apple pie coming from the kitchen. Carols on the radio sung by English boys with voices like clusters of perfect glass flowers. Chandeliers of sound.

> In the bleak mid-win-ter
> Frosty wind made moan

Yet each time the telephone went, her heart began to pound. She scolded it the way she might scold the cat or a child if it were impatient. "Don't be so silly." What had there been, really? A party, a letter written on yellow paper (a letter she had brought with her to read and read again). But there was something, she felt it, she was sure. There, the phone again. Let it ring. One. Two. Three. Then slowly pick it up.

"Hello. Oh hello, Mother — yes, of course. Wonderful. Perfectly all right.

On the afternoon of the 27th her youngest child arrived, laughing and triumphant.

"Do you realize that's the first time I've made that trip all by myself?"

"And you didn't get off at the wrong island. Good girl."

"I was pretty nervous. I'm supposed to phone Dad when we get home and let him know." She was enormously proud of herself.

They drove back up the island, chattering away. Was Tabitha still there? Oh yes. Had the sea-lions returned? Did she like her presents? Did Tabitha like the sardines?

"Yes," Martha said, "but I had to put up with sardine breath all afternoon." The road was slippery in places and the temperature was still dropping. It was nice to think of the cottage up there, waiting all snug and warm. Peter had taken the older children skiing; she and her youngest would have a few days alone.

The phone was ringing as they went up the path. Anne was in front and Martha tried not to hurry her. Although she'd given up, really. It would only be Peter, checking to see if Anne had made the trip all right. The phone stopped just as they opened the door.

"It was probably Peter," Martha said. "You'd better phone him." But the phone began again as she was speaking. Ring ring, ring ring.

"Hello," Anne said. Then, "It's for you. A *Man*." She gave her mother a funny look and went into the other room.

Martha wasn't sure at first; she had never heard his voice over the telephone and he sounded young and boyish.

"Merry Christmas," he said, and then, "is your New Year's offer still on? Anne and I were thinking we might come over."

Down goes the heart on its runaway elevator. You fool, did you really think he would be unattached?

"Anne?"

"My daughter. I told you I had a daughter."

"Oh yes, Anne. Your daughter. Of course. I don't think you told me her name."

"We thought we'd come on the morning ferry on the 31st and stay a few days."

"Lovely. I'll meet you."

"We could probably hitch a ride."

"I don't mind picking you up." She, who hated driving on icy roads, and the temperature was still dropping, *she* didn't mind. Mind? Why suddenly she had become a regular postman — through snow and sleet, et cetera, et cetera, et cetera.

"Hello," he said, "hello. Are you still there?" She thought he had hung up. Laughter. "Oh yes."

"Good. We'll see you soon."

Anne was in the front room playing with the cat.

"Can I sleep with you, Mum? This room is so much more cosy than mine when there's just me in it. Besides," she said, "mine's probably full of spiders."

"It is not. I did a spider check this morning and chucked them all outside. They will no doubt freeze to death and there will be spider corpses all over the snow."

"Ha. Ha. You can't guilt me. Anyway, I like to look at the little tree." A small one in a pot by the window, decorated with lights and gingerbread animals.

"It was crowding another tree," Martha said, "so I didn't feel bad about giving it the axe."

"Can we make some popcorn chains for the birds?"

"Tomorrow. I think that would be nice. But watch out for Tabby. Maybe keep her inside when you first string them up. She's old but she's awfully fast."

"Why do cats kill birds?"

"Instinct. Sport. Watch a cat play with a bird or a mouse it's caught. With a well-fed cat it certainly doesn't have much to do with hunger."

"You will have to stay inside," Anne said to the cat, who gazed at her through half-open eyes, "and be good." The cat purred.

When they were in bed and nearly asleep, the lights of the small tree reflected in the uncurtained window, the moonlight shining on the snow outside, Martha said, "A friend of mine is coming Friday morning."

"A friend of yours?"

"A new friend. His name is Richard. I think you'll like him." (Please like him, said the mother's heart to the child's. I like him. I like him a lot.) "He has a daughter, just about a year older than you."

"What's her name?"

"Anne, the same as yours. We'll have to call you Anne One and Anne Two."

Her daughter's voice was cold. "Nobody's going to want to be Anne Two."

(*Please*, said the mother's heart to the child's. What do you know about loneliness? Oh please.) "Well," she said, "we can call you Anne T. and her Anne L. No discrimination there."

"I thought we were going to be *alone*, over here," Anne said.

"We'll be alone tomorrow and the next day and the next," her mother said. "And then, on New Year's Eve, Richard and Anne L. will come and help us celebrate. I've even got some sparklers — from my stocking." She gave her daughter a hug. "It will be all right; it will be fun."

"We'll see," said the little girl. It was warm in the bed

with the two of them cuddled up to one another in their long flannel nightgowns, the cat asleep at their feet. Wasn't this enough, this warmth, this peace? Why had she invited two strangers in (ah, said her heart — you read his letter — can you really call such a man a stranger? Two *strangers*, she repeated firmly to her heart.) Why should the girls like one another? At that age — they were not really *little* girls any more — they weren't going to be content to play with dolls in another room while their parents talked. She could phone him in the morning, so sorry, change of plans, I'll write you when I get back.

Did the sea lions ever stop? Deep roars, barking — she's mine! She's mine! The young bulls battling the old bulls for supremacy. Did the females have any say in it at all? Or did the bull who won just give the female, the *cow*, a nudge, a push, and separate her from the herd? The fishermen hated them because they ate so many cod. Sometimes the fishermen shot them, which was against the law.

Down on the rocks, dragging their great bodies out of the sea, clumsy, not in their element, the old ritual went on. No guilt, no feelings of doubt, of failure, no letters, no phone calls, no meetings in coffee shops, no children who asked questions — just the annual struggle and dance and then it was over for that year. (But you wouldn't really want that, said her heart, would you?)

It thawed briefly and they made a snow family, including a cat. The snow cat had two green marbles for eyes and whiskers from the broom. The snow family wore clothes from the dressing-up box.

"We need lumps of coal," Martha said. "For eyes and mouths and buttons."

"Where did you get the ones you put in our Christmas boxes?"

"At a coal merchant's. When I told him what it was for, he let me have three pieces. Some people still burn coal in their fireplaces, but not many. Everybody had coal furnaces when I was growing up."

"It must have been nice when you were growing up," Anne said. She was painting on features with black poster paint. It ran a bit and the snow family all looked slightly weepy around the eyes.

"Nice for children, I guess. But there was a war on part of the time. Not so nice for grown-ups. And sometimes we children were even afraid. We heard things; we wondered."

She looked at her daughter, rosy-cheeked, healthy, concentrating on the snow-child's mouth.

"Are you ever afraid," Martha said, "about the possibility of war?"

"Sometimes. It's hard to really believe in it — that anybody would start a nuclear war."

"I know."

She did not tell her daughter how one night last month she had been listening to the radio in bed when the music suddenly went off and was replaced by a monotonous hum. No voice came on to announce technical difficulties. She had been sure the war had started and had thrown on her clothes. She wanted to be with her children; she was praying out loud to God to let her have time to get to the other side of the city, oh please, please —

And then the announcer's voice came on and the music began again. Something by Purcell, something old and beautiful. Half-dressed she sat on the bed and wept. She had not realized how deeply convinced she was that the madness could not be stopped.

"What are you going to make for tomorrow night, when *they* come?" Anne said.

"I thought I'd make pea soup, with the ham bone, and steamed brown bread."

"I'm not crazy about pea soup. Especially with those chillies in it — you make it so hot."

"Good. It will keep us all warm. Besides, I didn't bring an awful lot of food with me. I've got a chicken for New Year's Day and it's not very big. What would you like to have for New Year's Eve?"

"Something besides pea soup. Anyway, pea soup doesn't seem very — " She tried to think of the word.

"Festive?" her mother asked.

Anne nodded.

"Well, it's to have at midnight. We'll go for a walk just before midnight. Then we'll all come back and have pea soup."

"Some of us. Some of us will just shiver and starve."

"You can make grilled cheese sandwiches and cocoa."

"I wish we had a turkey carcass; then we could have turkey soup."

"Next year."

There was a pause. Anne turned a silver bracelet around and around on her arm.

"Did you open your presents all by yourself?"

"With Tabitha's help. I lit the fire and made a pot of coffee first, so I could get back in bed and open them in the warm." White lies. White and innocent as snow.

"I wish — " Anne said. The bracelet went round and round. (The child's heart spoke to the mother's heart. You don't know what it's like to be torn to pieces!)

"Shall we have a game of Chinese checkers?"

"I'll win," Anne said. The bracelet stopped its turning.

"Don't be so sure."

"Do you like pea soup?" Anne T. asked Anne L. in the back seat of the car. The ferry had been very late, because of strong winds, and eventually had come in at the other, more sheltered harbour. Martha was sure they would be cross and grumpy, but no, there they were, father and daughter, coming off the boat arm in arm, laughing.

"Here comes dinner!" he called. He was carrying a large, old-fashioned portmanteau. The girls were introduced. They all got into the car and headed back up the island.

"She doesn't like it!" Anne called. "She hates it."

"I didn't say that."

"I'm sure you were just being polite. We're going to have it at midnight. *Pea Soup*. There's two who don't like it," Anne called to her mother, laughing.

"Do you like pea soup?" Martha asked Richard. The road was slippery and she had to pay attention to her driving so she couldn't really look over at him.

"Love it."

"She puts chillies in it," Anne said.

"Even better."

"There's two who like it," Martha smiled at her daughter in the mirror.

"We've brought lots of things," Anne L. said. "A cottage roll and mandarin oranges and wine; and I have a whole box of home-made chocolates. My aunt has moulds and she showed me how to make them."

"Do you like school?" Anne T. asked.

"Some of it. I like Math."

"Oh I *hate* Math."

"But I don't like our French teacher. She's awful. She — "

"It's going to be all right," Martha said, very low, to Richard. "They like one another."

"But of course."

"It isn't always the case. Sometimes, when kids are thrown together — "

"Are you a worrier?" Richard said.

"Oh yes. I have a black belt in worrying. I worry," she said, "but sometimes I forget to do the things I'm worried about."

"For instance."

"For instance, I forgot to leave all the taps open last night. I worried that I'd forget, and I forgot. The pipes are frozen."

"All of them?"

"All. We have to melt snow for washing and washing up."

"Not too difficult," he said. "Not exactly a disaster."

"So long as the pipes don't burst."

"Stop it," Richard said.

"Do you like spiders?" Anne T. said to Anne L.

"I don't mind spiders but I hate eating eggs. They make me feel sick."

"What do you like?" Martha said to her companion.

"I like spiders and eggs. I like pea soup. I like New York in June. How about you?"

"Don't mind him," said Anne L., "he's a bit — you know." Lots of giggles from the back.

After the cottage had been examined and they'd all had lunch, they went to find the sea-lions. The girls ran on ahead. Everything sparkled — the world was made of mica, of coral. The two Annes had melted snow and poured it over the snow family to make them into ice sculptures. The water in the channel looked almost jellied.

"My God it's cold!" Richard said. But Martha stopped at the top of the hill, stopped and stood still.

"What's the matter, woman," Richard said, "you'll freeze if you don't keep moving."

She pulled the long wool scarf away from her face.

"Have you ever wanted to just stand still and laugh out loud or yell or do something like that? I'm so *happy.* Oh Richard, give me a kiss." She surprised herself by her daring.

"Our lips might stick together," he said, coming back and putting his arms around her.

"Somehow I don't think so." And then they carried on up the hill, arm in arm.

The girls were already down on the point, standing with a group of Blandings, also out for a walk. Mr Blanding lent them his binoculars.

"Why are all the sea-lions here?" Anne L. asked.

"They come here around this time every year, in order to mate."

The two girls looked at each other and giggled. Anne T. whispered something to Anne L. and they giggled some more.

"Would you like to stop in for a New Year's drink," Mrs Blanding said, eyeing Richard and his daughter. "The older kids are playing Monopoly; maybe the girls would like to join in."

"Could we come tomorrow?" Anne T. said. "We've got something to do this afternoon." Did she feel it too — that there was something fragile, something that she didn't want to share?

"We'll drop by tomorrow," Martha said.

"Or this evening," Mr Blanding suggested. Her favourite Blanding brother grinned at her.

"Possibly," Martha said.

Richard was watching the sea-lions through Mr Blanding's binoculars, stamping his feet from time to time in order to keep warm. He had on stout-looking brogues, but no boots.

"Amazing beasts," he said, handing back the glasses.

"Do they keep you awake?" Mrs Blanding asked Martha.

"The first night they did. Or rather, they woke me up."

"Well, the old bulls won't give in without a fight," Mr Blanding said. "Although a lot of it is just threats, just noise."

"We counted seventy of them yesterday," Mrs Blanding said. She moved so that she was standing next to Martha.

"Are you having a nice holiday?"

"Oh yes. Very nice thank you."

"Mother," Anne called from the children's room. "I'm going to sleep on the top bunk and give Anne L. the bottom."

"That's fine." And no problem switching from the bed in the front room. So long as it was Anne's idea, not hers. Richard was sitting in one of the old easy chairs, the cat on his lap. His feet were bare, as were hers. The girls had painted everyone's fingernails and toenails with green nail polish. Martha had drawn the line at the cat. Richard had small bones; Martha thought his feet were beautiful. She sat facing him, on the carpet, in front of the stove. It was almost midnight.

"Did you bring sleeping bags?" she said.

"Bag," Richard said, looking at her with a small smile, his hand stroking the cat's head and continuing down her back, stroking, stroking. "I brought a sleeping bag for Anne. I thought perhaps I could sleep with you."

Martha smiled and opened the door of the stove, gave the fire a poke. Her cheeks were so hot.

"There ought to be a special phrase book," she said, "for the country of the human heart."

"We're doing all right," Richard said, "without it."

"Shut your eyes," Anne T. called, "here we come."

They were dressed up in lace curtains and bits of cloth from the old dressing-up box. And tons of make-up — eyes, lips, cheeks.

"My goodness," Martha said.

"Who are these visions?" Richard asked.

Martha had tuned the radio to a program of Acadian music. Anne T. went over and fiddled with the dials. "That music doesn't suit our costumes; we want to dance."

"I don't think you'll get anything very oriental tonight," Richard said. But she found a program of Hit Songs from Yester-year and the two girls began to dance, slowly, to "Love Letters in the Sand."

"That's a *real* oldie," Martha said. "My father used to sing that when he was driving." The two girls swayed, joined hands, moved apart, lost in some private dream of their own. Then the music stopped abruptly and switched to "Auld Lang Syne."

"Oh," Martha said. She ran to the kitchen for the champagne. "Put your coats and boots on," she called. "We can light the sparklers on the porch."

Richard opened the champagne and they all rushed

outside. They could hear firecrackers somewhere and a man's voice calling Happy New Year.

"Happy New Year," Martha said. She kissed her daughter, then Anne L. and then Richard. They all clinked glasses. Watched the sparklers hiss and glitter. "I've got to go inside," Martha said. "My slippers are too thin."

"Get your boots and come back out."

"No, it's lovely but it's too cold."

"We old folks are going inside," Richard said, "*and* taking the champagne."

"Can we take the rest of the sparklers and go down on the Government Wharf?"

"If you put caps on and if you don't fall in and drown."

They flew down the path, long dresses dragging underneath their coats.

"I don't think youth is wasted on the young," Martha said. "Who else could keep up with it? I'm going to pour some of that melted snow into a kettle and make them hot-water bottles — I think they'll need them."

When she came back into the front room, Richard dished out the soup and poured them each another glass of champagne.

"They've already had their grilled cheese," Martha said, "But they might want some cocoa."

"Don't fuss; they can get it."

The two Annes burst in the door — "It's too cold! We lit one but then we couldn't stand it. We put it out in the snow. Can we have some more champagne?"

"Put your night-gowns and slippers on and bring a pan of milk. We'll heat it up for some cocoa."

Great giggling in the other room and a firm drawing of the curtain. Back they came in their night-gowns,

still in full make-up. Anne L. sat on the carpet with her
head against her father's knee, his hand in her hair. The
other Anne lay full length, by her mother. After the
cocoa had been drunk, they went to bed.

"Dad."

"Daddykins."

"Richard!"

"Come kiss us goodnight!" Richard went into the
other room. Martha could hear his quiet voice, hear
their giggles.

"Mum."

"Mummykins."

"Martha!"

It was her turn to kiss them.

"Would you leave the candle burning for a little
while and then come back and blow it out?"

"No," Martha said, "I'm going to bed now. It's very
bright in here with the moonlight and the stars." She
picked up the candlestick and looked at herself in the
mirror. "Haven't I seen you somewhere before?" she
said to the woman in the wavering glass. Then she blew
out the candle, licked her fingers and pinched the wick.

"Good-night my dears, Happy New Year."

"Good-night, good-night."

Richard had built up the fire and closed down the
vents.

"Does the cat stay in or out?" he said.

"In, when it's this cold. Unless it bothers you."

"So long as she stays at the bottom of the bed."

"She will."

"I feel terribly shy," Martha said, lighting the candle by
the bed, turning off the light.

"You have no monopoly on shyness," he said. He

began to take off his clothes. Martha turned her back and pulled her sweater over her head.

"What the — !"

Martha turned around.

"There's something the matter with the Goddamned bed. I can't get in." He stood there, naked and cross in the candlelight.

Martha turned back the covers.

"They've apple-pied the bed."

"They've what?"

"Apple-pied, short-sheeted. Didn't you ever do that when you were young?"

"The little brats."

"It'll only take a minute to fix; it's just the top sheet."

Standing naked, one on either side of the bed, they remade the bed.

"We'll get you guys tomorrow," Richard called softly to the other room. No reply. They got into bed.

"Oh God, Martha, your feet are cold."

"Cold feet, warm heart."

"I think it's supposed to be cold hands."

"My hands are cold as well."

"Here, give them to me. I'll warm them."

"You're so warm you're like a furnace."

Whisperings and murmurings, whisperings and murmurings. The wood in the stove falls, rearranges itself, flares up, makes pretty patterns on the ceiling.

"Well, at least *my* pipes aren't frozen."

"That feels good."

"What?"

"Your hand on my thigh."

"Happy New Year, Richard."

"Happy New Lang Syne."

"Good-night."

"Good-night."

But she couldn't sleep, couldn't quite relax. Where was this going to lead? Who would leave first?

Richard spoke into her ear. "I can hear your mind whirring around. Turn it off.

"I can't."

"Of course you can."

She smiled to herself in the darkness.

"I had a book when I was a child," she said, "called *The Little Engine That Could*. Do you know that story?"

"Nope."

"It's about a small engine that is teased by the big engines in the round-house and then finally he gets to pull a heavy load. He puffs along saying I-think-I-can/ I-think-I-can/ I-think-I-can/ I think I can I think I can...."

"You *guys!*" Her daughter's voice from the other room.

"Shut up, Mum," Richard said. He held her tight.

After a little while all slept.

Compulsory Figures

Compulsory Figures

There are twenty-six bones in the foot. That is the alphabet of the foot. Let us consider the tarsus, or ankle, with its seven bones. The placement of the ankle allows him to stand upright. Then there is the metatarsus, with its five long metatarsals and the toes, or phalanges, with their fourteen bones. The big toe has two bones, connected at the joint, but each of the other toes has three.

The toes are important for balance.

The muscles of the foot control the movement of the toes. All the other movements of the foot are controlled by the muscles of the leg.

It is the big toe he likes best. On the wall of his basement apartment there are drawings based on illustrations found in encyclopedias and Gray's *Anatomy*: the foot seen from the left side, the foot seen from the right. There are precise drawings of the bones of the foot of the dog (who walks on his toes), of the horse (who walks on his one remaining toe).

Leg bones — tibias and fibulas — do not interest him. Only once in his life has he been on snowshoes but he thought to himself that this was how a bird must feel, walking across the top of the snow. He loved it.

When he was small his mother always bought him Thom McCann shoes. Twice a year they went to the shoe department of the town's only department store, where first he was measured with a thing called a Baxter Device, a heavy metal adjustable sole which showed how long his foot was and how wide; and then he stepped up onto a platform and thrust his feet into the X-ray machine. Looking down, he could see all his footbones, the flesh fallen away, swimming in orderly formation in a sea of milky green. Until he left school and got a job, his shoes were the only new things he ever had. The first night he always slept with them under his pillow.

His mother worked hard. His father went away to the war and came back not exactly crazy, but changed. Sometimes, at the end of the day, his mother gave him a nickel to massage her feet. She wore men's carpet slippers on her feet because they were so swollen.

His father wasn't allowed to drive because he had developed something like epilepsy after he came back from the war. One day he was on the bus with his father, who began talking in a loud voice to a woman across the aisle.

"Everybody thinks I'm crazy," he said. "They say I am, and maybe I am, but I know something that they don't know. I've got the mind of a little girl that died. When they sent me up to Spokane to see that specialist, he put me on a table and stuck some needles in my head but wouldn't let me see what he was doing. Just made me lay there with my head covered up for a long time. I just layed there and never said a word, but they had this little girl there at the time, who died. What they did was when they had those needles in my head, they put her brain in my head, at least the nerve section."

The woman smiled and stared intently at the back of the bus driver's shoulders.

"It's true," his father insisted. "I felt her mind coming, so I just took a deep breath and let it come. She came on in like she'd been there forever. I even have her dreams — little girl dreams." He never heard his father mention the little girl again.

But his mother was a saint. She also made the best buttermilk pancakes he had ever tasted. If a visitor came for Sunday supper, she would get out her big black griddle and start frying pancakes. He and his brothers and sisters would be almost hysterical with anticipation, especially if it was a new person, somebody who hadn't been to Sunday supper before. Mama would stand up by the old stove with her back to the table, pick up a pancake with her pancake turner and toss it high in the air. It would go whosh, whosh, across the room, spinning and twirling and come to land SMACK in the middle of the visitor's plate. Even his Daddy had to laugh at that.

She could sing, too. She knew lots of hymns and songs.

> Oh you can't get to Heaven
> (oh you can't get to Heaven)
> In a rockin' chair
> (in a rockin' chair)
> 'Cause the Lord don't 'low
> ('cause the Lord don't 'low)
> No lazy folks there.

Once, while they were all singing and stomping about in the kitchen, his father got up from his chair by the window, took a jelly glass down off the shelf and flung it at the wall. There were little splinters of glass everywhere — like frozen rain.

His mother stopped in the middle of a word. "Oh Honey," she said, "Oh Honey. What'd you want to go and do that for?" Then quite calmly, without sweeping anything up, she began another song:

(them bones them bones
gonna
Walk around
them bones them bones
gonna
Walk around
them bones them bones gonna
Walk around
now hear the word of the Lord)

He was not interested in the feet of young girls, in their high-heeled shoes with flimsy straps. He liked experienced feet, feet that had been intimate with hard work and pavements and pain. For a while he had worked in a big hospital as an orderly — he had asked to be put on the old people's ward. He trembled as he bathed the feet of old inarticulate men; he read whole paragraphs from the gnarled bones beneath their pale binding of skin. But he was never allowed to bathe the women — certainly not. Only the doctors and interns and female nurses were ever allowed to touch the women, even the very old ones, the ones beyond sex, beyond death almost but not quite, the ones who whispered in parched voices, "Doctor, let me die."

His lawyer did not understand at all. He was making a joke of everything; the whole courtroom was laughing while he stood there, staring at his shoes. The lawyer said it was like grabbing a good-night kiss. The people in the courtroom rocked with laughter.

He had studied the foot. He knew everything — almost — there was to know about the foot. He had seen tired women at bus stops at the end of the day, shifting their weight from one foot to another, and he longed to kneel down in front of them, to massage their feet and worship them. He saw the pinched bones beneath their ill-fitting shoes. His hands shook with longing and with pity. The tips of his fingers burned.

The lawyer told the judge that his client was only trying to get to know the women better.

The first time was in a shoe store.

The second was at an Open House.

The third — — —

He knelt before them and began massaging their feet.

The lawyer told him there was a criminal charge, that the women had charged him with something called common assault. When he looked blank, the lawyer said that, in law, this was the "least form of touching."

He still didn't understand. He saw the jelly glass shatter against the kitchen wall. He heard his mother's voice: "Oh Honey, what'd you want to go and do that for?"

Even the judge was smiling as he levied the fine. But it was an assault, he said; it was not like grabbing a good-night kiss at all. "Six hundred dollars," the judge said. "Six hundred dollars."

He had picked up a foot measure that wasn't being

used, a Baxter Device. And had approached the woman calmly, speaking in a gentle voice.

"Good afternoon, may I help you?" He placed her foot in the measure and moved the slide up and down up and down. "What beautiful feet you have," he murmured. "Your feet are so beautiful." Almost absent-mindedly he began to massage her toes.

"What are you doing?" she cried.

He gave a little gasp, almost a sob.

"I'm sorry," he said, releasing her. "Give me the shoe you want I will find it in your size." Then he picked up his overcoat from a neighbouring chair and walked quickly out of the store.

"It's not funny," he says to the judge. "There's nothing to laugh about."

The foot is essential for locomotion. Taking him firmly by the arm, the lawyer leads him out of the courtroom. The lawyer is something of a wit. He cannot resist saying, loud enough for everybody to hear, "Cheer up, old boy, that's not too bad. That's only sixty dollars a toe! Not bad, not bad at all."

What is he going to do now? What on earth is he going to do?

Mothering Sunday

Mothering Sunday

Hail Mary, Wounded art Thou among Women. That's what it means, doesn't it? Still, there in the French: *blesser*: to harm, to hurt, to injure, to wound. "*C'était une blessure grave.*" *Se blesser*, to wound oneself. In English we can trace the word back to *blōd*. Hail Mary, Blessed art Thou among Women. All the Marys bleed.

I am sitting here in this elegant French restaurant, surrounded by mothers and daughters, mothers and sons, mothers and sons and daughters-in-law (who probably rang up and made the reservations and arranged for the corsage). Not many children around but then, this is not the kind of restaurant where one takes young children, not North American children. Families with young children are no doubt celebrating at McDonalds or Smitty's Pancake House. I had forgotten it was Mother's Day when I arranged to meet Lydia at this restaurant and I, as usual, was early. She, as usual, is very late. Perhaps she missed her train connection and will not show up at all. I'd hate to miss her

— I'm hardly ever in Toronto — but sitting here surrounded by all these mothers is dreadful. Should I hold
up a sign: I AM A MOTHER TOO or stand up and
show my stretch marks? But then they would think — if
she is a mother where are her children. Why is she
sitting alone, corsageless, with no one to buy her an
"Anna M" cocktail, concocted in honour of Anna M.
Jarvis, the founder, foundress, of Mother's Day in
America. A little card on the table explains the whole
thing. Anna M. never had children of her own and died
penniless and almost sightless, in a quiet sanitorium in
Pennsylvania at the age of eighty-four. She devoted her
life to Mother's Day and to her blind sister Elsinore. I
wonder about Anna M.'s mother, naming a daughter
Elsinore, especially when the other gets a common-
garden name like Anna M. Something rotten in the
State of Pennsylvania! "In a quiet sanitorium in Pennsylvania." I've worked in those places. Hardly quiet.
Noisy and rowdy and the old ladies coming out with
words you could hardly believe, throwing balls of shit at
one another, puddles forming under their chairs. I
didn't mind. I was young; it would never happen to me.
I wonder if there were at least two pennies in her purse,
to shut her eyes.

Several of the mothers are sipping their Anna M.
cocktails — they look like Harvey Wallbangers. I am sipping white wine. I wish Lydia would hurry up; she and
I are good together, we make each other laugh, egg each
other on to say more and more outrageous things. The
young no-hipped waiter (imagine *him* giving birth to
anything bigger than a jelly baby) would be very quickly
demolished by a combination of Lydia and myself.
When he suggested an Anna M. cocktail Lydia would
ask for a Bloody Mary or a glass of milk, as being
more appropriate for the occasion. Who first came up

with *that* name, Bloody Mary? Businessmen ordering it
on airplanes without batting an eye, if you gave them a
glass of blood they'd reach for the sick-bags pretty
quickly. Or Bloody Caesar, who, like MacDuff was from
his mother's womb untimely ripp'd. No blood, no
bloody Mary in the nativity accounts. Immaculate con-
ception, immaculate delivery. We mothers know better,
sitting here with our legs underneath the table, sitting
here sipping our drinks, picking at the expensive food.
Blood. A heavy word. No blood for months and then a
lot. All cleaned up, fresh straw, fresh clothes, by the time
the Wise Men came. In our church there was always a
Christmas pageant and a white gift service on a Sunday
near to Christmas. Children playing Mary, Joseph,
Angels, Shepherds, Wise Men. "Gifts" for the poor
children wrapped in white tissue paper and laid in
front of the *tableau vivant*. All the parents loved it,
especially the mothers. All the mothers wanted their
daughters to be Mary.

The other day a young woman told me that, if you
have the sperm, you can impregnate yourself with a
turkey baster. I laughed and laughed and she was hurt.
It was the turkey baster that made me laugh. Birds still
involved in immaculate conceptions. Turkeys, such
large, stupid delicate birds. Raised to be devoured at
times of Thanksgiving and praise. Hail turkey, blessed
art thou amongst birds. Turkeys didn't come completely
dressed (meaning undressed) when I was a kid; my
mother sat in the kitchen pulling out pin feathers
after she had singed the bird, holding it over a candle,
turning it. The kitchen smelled of burning feathers.

What do you do? Squirt the turkey-baster up you and
then stand on your head for half an hour? (I don't
really want to know.)

Where is Lydia? She knows the name of the

restaurant, why hasn't she phoned? I could leave and go back to my hotel and wait for her there I guess; but I'm hungry and it's Sunday. We can't buy a bottle of wine and take it up to my room.

There are two carnations, one red, one white, in a crystal vase at each table. I wonder why it's always carnations — something to do with incarnate perhaps? The Word made flesh? That's another memory from my childhood, women standing on the church steps after the Mother's Day service, women wearing corsages of white or red carnations. White if the mother were dead, red if she were alive. But I don't remember us ever giving our mother a corsage of carnations. She probably told us not to. She had a habit of telling us not to do things: not to give her candy on Valentine's Day, not to give her birthday presents. I think now it was her way of asking for them but I didn't understand then. I understand, now, a great deal more about mothers. How they weren't, perhaps still aren't, supposed to ask for things. Unless they are useful of course — washing machines or microwave ovens.

Was Jesus a difficult child? Did he have tantrums, nightmares? Did he wet the bed? The Holy Ghost, the Original Big Bird, descends on her while she is sleeping and she wakes up pregnant.

(Lydia would probably add, "with maybe a spot of bird shit on the sheet.")

The original surrogate mother, and she doesn't even get to name the child. I wonder if he was a cult figure after he started preaching, he and his gang of twelve. We know that Mary and the other women followed him and the apostles "ministering" to them. But did the women steal bits of his clothes or snippets of hair, did they fight over who was going to bake the bread or hand him the honeycomb?

I think I'm a little oppressed by all this Mother's Day stuff, special drinks, special flowers. Shall I stay or shall I go? I don't feel neglected. When I get back home next week there will be cards and probably flowers, promises of breakfast in bed. But just now, alone in a room full of mothers and children I have some sense of what it must be like for those who never had children, never had that clear proof of their female-ness. See! See! I'm a mother; at least I've done something with my life. "Ocular proof."

Lydia's mother died when Lydia was fifteen. We talked about it once, whether that affected her and if so in what ways. Lydia ran the house for her father and younger brothers and sisters. She remembers her mother in a red-checked housedress with a big white collar. And a bib-apron over that. She was English and she wrote a lot of letters home. In England Mother's Day is called Mothering Sunday. She always wanted to send flowers to England on Mothering Sunday but never had the money. She died without ever seeing England or her mother again.

Lydia remembers that her mother cut out poems by Edna Jacques and stuck them on the ice-box. Lydia was very funny about Edna Jacques the Poet Laureate of the Kitchen. Even Nellie McClung admired her. The poems had titles like "A Mother at Night," "Small Deeds" and "A Mother at Christmas." I grew up in the States and had never heard of Edna Jacques. I think we had a similar person called Audrey Alexandra Brown. Last year Lydia found a copy of one of Edna Jacques's books in a second-hand store and gave it to me for my birthday. It's full of words like *bounteous* and *mayhap* and *laughter-tinted song*. The trouble is that although I laugh at Edna Jacques she does understand something about the wonder of watching little children. I've saved locks of

"golden" hair, and early drawings, even a Mother's Day
card from one of them

HAPY   M
OTHERS   DAY

I have no right to laugh at Edna Jacques.

I grew up during the Second World War. Mothers
hung little silk flags in the front-room windows: a blue
star on the flag if your son was fighting overseas, a gold
star if he were killed or missing in action. Gold stars, in
elementary school, were given for the very best, perfect
or nearly perfect work. The teacher hung gold-star
papers around the room. So gold-star mothers, and they
were called that reverently, "Gold Star Mothers" were
the perfect mothers, who had given up their sons to
make the world safe for democracy. They would not
have seen how they were part of the great myth, the old
lie.

(I have just ordered another carafe of the house wine
and some pâté and bread. "My friend has been
delayed," I said brightly to my pretty no-hipped waiter.
He doesn't believe me; he thinks I am a rejected
Mother. He frowned when I ordered more wine. "It's all
right," I said. "I'm not an alcoholic, I'm a drinker."
Lydia will be here soon — she has never let me down.
None of her children are at home any more, but
perhaps she had an unexpected long distance call and
missed the train. You can't cut people off when they've
taken the trouble to phone you long distance.)

I went to see my mother last week. She is eighty-nine
years old and lives in a cosy apartment in a senior
citizens' complex near Boston. Every time I visit now
she gives me something or shows me something that is
"coming to me" after she dies. This time it was two

lovely fans, one red silk and lace, one black, which had
belonged to her mother. They are very fragile and I
shall have to open them out, mount them and then
frame them. Very fragile and very exotic, from a time
when women carried fans on special occasions. We
looked at old photographs and talked a bit, drank tea.
Then in one box of bits and pieces which are to go to
my sister and me my eye lit on a large oval frame, of
some beautiful dark wood, cherry wood perhaps. I
asked her what had been in it — I didn't remember it
at all. She said, "Oh, do you want it? I was going to
throw that away." I asked again whose picture the frame
had been for. She said, "My mother." I asked her where
the picture was now. She said, "I tore it up." Then she
took the frame out of my hands and put it away in a
drawer. She didn't offer the frame to me again.

Why? What had her mother done? I had always
thought she loved her mother. I couldn't ask. It was
something terrible and private, something between
mothers and daughters, something Edna Jacques would
never write about, the dark side of all this, the wounds
as well as blessings.

"Well," I said, "I must be going now." I could see that
she was tired, that we had run out of safe things to talk
about. I have wounded her many times; she has
wounded me. We don't talk about this. We send each
other letters and greeting cards and presents; we worry
about one another. We wonder.

"Well," I said, putting on my coat, "I'll write to you
soon." We kissed the air and then she walked me to the
front entrance. She looks twenty years younger than she
really is. Women her age move through the over-heated
halls pushing walkers or shaking with those hidden
winds of extreme age.

"Goodbye," we call to one another through the

glass door. "Goodbye, goodbye."

Here's Lydia coming in, shaking her umbrella, laughing. She sees me and waves.

"Don't have the Anna M. Jarvis cocktail," I say as she sits down, breathless and laughing. She smiles up at the waiter.

"What about a Bloody Mary?" and winks at me.

One of the mothers is celebrating her birthday. Her waiter is bringing in a cake. The whole restaurant starts singing, takes up the tune.

"Happy Birthday, Dear Mother, Happy Birthday to you."

"I missed the train," Lydia says, then looks around. "My God, look at all the mothers!"

"Did you bronze your children's baby shoes?"

"No, no. We didn't have the money. But I was definitely of the bronzed shoe school."

"Me too. Did you save things?"

"Boxes and boxes of things. But I wasn't as bad as a woman up the street. She saved all her children's milk teeth in a glass jar on the kitchen counter."

"Listen Lydia, I want to tell you something that just happened with my mother. Only let's order first. I'm starving."

We signal the waiter to bring the menus. I pour another glass of wine and begin.

The Princess and
the Zucchini

The Princess and
the Zucchini

This is the way it happened:

There had been a long, hot summer and the Royal Garden was full to overflowing. The gardeners were hot and grumpy and said they could not keep up with all the picking. Everybody was hot and grumpy, even the King, even the Queen and especially Princess Zona, who stood now, in her long white night-dress, gazing down at the garden below her, glowing silver in the moonlight. She hadn't been able to sleep at all, because of the heat, and wished with all her heart for a thunderstorm and a downpour to break the pressure of the night. It had not rained in weeks and except for the garden, which was watered carefully every evening as soon as the sun had left it, the rest of the royal estate was parched and brown.

The garden looked inviting; she wanted to walk in the garden with bare feet. She opened the door quietly and tiptoed past the bedroom of her sleeping parents, tiptoed to the royal staircase, and went quietly and carefully down, down, down, then along corridors and passages, the moonlight streaming in through leaded windows, until she reached the kitchen, then the pantry, then the back door. The door creaked a little when she opened it and she heard a mouse jump in one of the cupboards. Then she was out, running across the dry lawn, which tickled her feet, and through the white gate into the garden. The paths were cool and moist; the air was fragrant; her long blonde hair glittered and gleamed in the moonlight. It was very still.

"I could sleep out here," she thought. "I could get one of the gardeners to sling me up a hammock. I wish I'd thought of it sooner." She didn't want to go back up to her hot stuffy little room, pretty as it was. She wished, at least, that she had brought something to sit on.

And then, because she wasn't really paying attention, she tripped and stubbed her toe on a large zucchini.

"Thank God," a deep voice said. The princess froze in fear.

"Who's there?" she whispered, trembling. "What do you want?"

"Here," the voice said. It came from beside her and below.

"Where?" She thought of all the old stories of dwarfs and elves and gnomes. There must be a dwarf hiding in the vines. Her curiosity got the better of her fear.

"Come out where I can see you," she said. "It's so overgrown in here, I can't really see you at all."

"You're looking right at me," the deep voice said.

"I'm sorry. I may be 'looking right at' you, but I still can't see you. Are you invisible or something?"

There was a deep, green groan.

"Would that it were that simple," the voice sighed.

"I'm the zucchini you just stubbed your toe against."

"Don't be ridiculous."

"It's true."

"I'm not in the mood for jokes," she said, and drawing herself up to her full height of four feet eleven inches and mustering all the dignity she could muster, standing there in her summer nightie, she demanded:

"Come out of there right now!"

"I wish I could," said the voice. "If you would kiss me, then I could."

"How can I kiss you when I don't know where you are?"

"I told you, I'm the zucchini."

"Are you a ventriloquist?" she said. "Are you a shape-shifter?"

"Neither of those," said the voice. "I'm a handsome young prince who has been cast under a wicked, wicked spell."

The princess laughed merrily; the laugh sounded like the tinkle of crystal chandeliers. She clapped her hands.

"I understand it all now. This is just one of those crazy dreams I have sometimes. Like the time I dreamt I had a conversation with my horse. Or the time I dreamt I was a mermaid living underneath the sea. When I wake up tomorrow, I'll tell Mother. She always asks about my dreams."

"If you think this is a dream, why don't you try and wake yourself up?"

"That's true. I usually can, when I realize I'm dreaming." She shut her eyes tight and willed herself awake.

"It won't work, will it?" said the zucchini.

It wouldn't work. When she opened her eyes, she was

not lying in her own little brass bed but was standing upright in the midnight garden.

"There's some mistake. This has to be a dream."

"A nightmare for me, maybe," said the voice, "but not a dream for you."

"Whoever heard of a prince being turned into a zucchini! A bear, yes; a swan, certainly; even a frog, although personally I find that one a little hard to swallow. But a vegetable! That's utterly ridiculous. Somebody's pulling my leg."

"Nobody's pulling your leg. I was standing in this garden one night, very late, gazing up at the light in your little window, trying to get up enough nerve to sing you a song I'd composed about your beauty, when all of a sudden I felt very strange, as though I'd faint if I didn't lie down; so I did that and the next thing I knew I was a tiny zucchini."

The princess laughed and laughed.

"You're not tiny now!"

"No. I grow bigger and bigger every day. It's all this watering and sunlight. I'm afraid I may burst."

"What makes you so sure that if I kiss you, you'll turn back into a prince?"

"Isn't your name Zona?"

"Yes it is. But I didn't choose it. It's a family name. The women in our family have always been called Zona. God knows why. I don't like it. As soon as I'm of age, I'm going to change it to Suzanne."

"I think it's a lovely name," the zucchini said. "I come from a land far away across the sea and I heard your name, fell in love with your name, long before I saw your portrait. I travelled for a year and a day to get here, saying your name softly to myself as I went, weary and wind-lashed, 'Zona, Zona, Zona,' to keep my courage up."

"But why does that convince you that I can save you? Love doesn't really conquer all and, even if it did, I'm not in love with you, it's the other way around."

"Don't you see? I've been changed into something beginning with the letter *Z*. Your name begins with *Z*. It must be a sign. I'm sure that only someone whose name begins with *Z* can save me."

"And if it's me and if my kiss can save you, what then?"

"What then! You know what then. 'Happily ever after.'"

"I don't think I could stand the idea of kissing a zucchini — it's so bizarre. What if somebody saw me!"

"Think about it for a while, but hurry."

"I am thinking about it; the idea repulses me." Then she added, "I have to go in now, I'm getting sleepy."

"Oh please Zona," the zucchini cried. "Just one little kiss."

"I'll think about it. Anyway, I'll come see you tomorrow night."

"I may have burst by then," he said sadly.

"Oh, I don't think so. And if you do, it will prove you're not really a prince, won't it?"

"How cruel you are!" he murmured.

"Just practical," she replied, and ran back the way she had come.

The next morning it all seemed like a very silly dream. Nevertheless, she went out right after breakfast and stuck a little hand-lettered sign in front of the zucchini. "PLEASE DON'T PICK THIS ZUCCHINI" it said. "BY ORDER OF H.R.H. PRINCESS ZONA." She had lessons to do, so she didn't stop to chat, just stuck a broken bean pole through the sign and pushed it into the moist earth near the vine. "I'll come back tonight," she whispered, hoping none of the gardeners would overhear her.

It wasn't a dream. The zucchini really had talked to her, really had told her his sad tale of woe. Every evening, close to midnight, the young princess walked up and down between the bean rows, the ripe tomatoes, the broccoli and cucumbers until she reached the back of the garden where the zucchinis grew. There she sat on a cushion and listened to stories of life in the distant land from which the prince — if he was a prince — had come. He had a deep, thrilling voice and she came to look forward eagerly to his accounts of his adventures.

But she would not kiss him; she absolutely refused.

"Have you no pity?" he cried. "Have you no heart?"

"I don't quite understand it myself," she admitted. "Something keeps holding me back. At the risk of sounding offensive, I think it really does have to do with the fact that you are a zucchini. What kind of spell is that? There's something not quite noble about it somehow."

He laughed bitterly. "Do you think the Frog Prince found it 'noble' to be a frog?"

"I suppose he didn't. But that's another story and another princess; it's nothing to do with me." She sighed. "Since you have to go through all this — and I still don't understand who could have done it to you — why couldn't you have been changed into an eagle, or a swan, or a chestnut stallion?"

"Well I wasn't. I was standing in a vegetable garden and I was changed into a garden vegetable. That's just the way it was."

"Well it's too bad you weren't standing by the peacocks or at the stable door."

"Ha ha." He paused. "Sometimes you're not very nice to me, you know. I suffer horribly."

"How can I be nice to you when 'you' is only a voice? I must admit, however, that the voice is very beautiful."

"Doesn't it make you want to see the rest?"

"Yes, no, oh — I don't know! Don't rush me."

"I can't get much bigger, Zona. I feel that if you don't release me, then I'll die."

"Tell me again about the 'Happily ever after.'"

The rains had still not come and everyone seemed to exist in a kind of terrible tension. The King snapped at the Queen, the Queen snapped at Zona, Zona snapped at everybody. One night she sat at her dressing table brushing her long golden hair and thinking. She tried to imagine the young prince before he had been changed into a zucchini. She tried to imagine happily ever after.

"Ninety-eight — ninety-nine — one hundred," she said, and put down the hairbrush. She stared at herself in the mirror. The zucchini had told her she was the most beautiful girl he had ever seen. Her mother and father told her she was beautiful. Her mirror said the same thing.

"But who is the 'I' who is so beautiful," she thought.

"Who is she? I will be fifteen next month. That's a lot of Ever After."

She sat in her night-dress, with her hands in her lap, long after her candle had sputtered and gone out. She sat like that, in the darkness, far into the night.

It had finally rained, and the King and Queen and Princess Zona were smiling as they dined *en famille* and listened to the blessed sound of the rain on the castle roof. It was the cook's day off and Zona had begged her mother to let her prepare the evening meal.

"Absolutely delicious," said the King, wiping his bowl with a piece of bread. "What did you say it was again?"

"Ratatouille," Zona said. "I found the receipe in *The Joy of Cooking.*"

"It really is very very good, dear," said the Queen. "We'll have to have it again."

The King and Queen smiled at one another tenderly.

"Our little girl is growing up," said the King.

"It won't be long," said the Queen, "before she'll be having boyfriends."

Zona smiled at them both and offered the dish around a second time.

One Size Fits All

One Size Fits All

It started with the dreams. Something had gone wrong in my life. Somebody was going going gone.

The dreams were full of fog. Out of the fog a face appeared and spoke to me. One phrase each night, that's all. The first two phrases were like messages in fortune cookies or in those old-fashioned weight machines. The third was very strange.

The first said

EXPECT CHANGES

The second said

AVOID SCANDAL

The Third said

EVERYTHING MUST GO

After that I gave up dreaming. Then things began to appear on my kitchen table. The first thing was a straw. Attached to the straw by a piece of red thread was a tiny label. It said:

THIS IS THE LAST STRAW

The second day I found on the table a dirty piece of rope. It too had a label, attached with a piece of yellow thread. The label said:

YOU'RE AT THE END OF YOUR TETHER

The third morning there was a measuring cup on the table, one of those cups that are marked on the side with both ounces and millilitres. It was full right up to the brim. There was a label attached to the handle by a green thread.

YOU'VE HAD IT UP TO HERE

So I decided to go to Kingston, Ontario. That is what people do when their lives fall apart in their hands like a badly bound book. Or that is what some people do. Well, anyway, it's what I did.

I called the nice man at Via Rail. He told me I could go on the *Rapido* at eleven o'clock the next morning. Before I knew it, I would be in Kingston. He gave me a number and some letters to quote when I went to pick up my ticket. "*W* for William," he said, "Z for Zulu."

"Z for Zulu," I enquired. "Do you make these up?"

"Oh no," he said. "Z for Zulu is a standard reply. We are taught very carefully what to say for each letter. We have it drummed into us." I liked the idea of the man who had Zulu drummed into him. It made me smile.

The *Rapido* pulled out precisely at 11 A.M. The coach I was in was very cold in spite of the fact, or perhaps because of it, that the temperature in Toronto was over one hundred degrees. The taxi driver had said "How do you like this heat?" and I said "It's too hot for me" and he said "You women are all alike. You don't want to perspire." Now I was too cold. There was a note at the bottom of the timetable. It said: "Checked handbaggage only. Human remains and pets not handled." It was cold enough, surely, for human remains? I could feel my heart freezing over. Soon it would be nothing but a lump of bright red ice. I had looked forward to this journey and now here I was freezing to death between Toronto and Kingston. Life is certainly full of nasty little surprises.

I managed to get off at Kingston without breaking. I took a taxi into town and went straight to the Prince George Hotel. There were lots of old buildings made of grey limestone blocks. There were multitudes locked up inside those buildings. My heart went out to them. It's hard work being crazy — on your feet all day with your ear pressed to the shell of the world. It's very noisy.

The desk clerk at the hotel said that my friend was waiting. I said there must be some mistake. "Oh no," he said, "he's out there on the porch. Go out and join him. I will get the waitress to bring you something cool in a tall glass."

I did not know which one was my friend so I went and sat down at a small white table. Across the street the tourist train was about to take off. Lots of tourist mothers and fathers and tourist children, very hot and grumpy, were climbing aboard. They all had pale puffy bodies and wore strange clothes, the kind of clothes you are given when you leave a certain type of hospital and they say "Goodbye Dear, good luck, keep your chin up."

A man sat down across from me. Perhaps this was my friend.

"That train was made by the prisoners," he said.

"You should take a trip on it. It's lots of fun."

Great truckloads of soldiers in spotted uniforms went by.

"Special Services," he whispered. "Well we know *we're* whoring," he said, "but at least our hymens will grow back." He showed me pictures of his family and his dog.

"I have a ghost child," I said. "She says to me Mama, do you love me

and I say yes

and she says Mama, do you love me?

and I say yes

but no matter how often I say it, she won't stay with me for very long. No matter how much power I sprinkle on my words she'll never stay. Her ghost Mama stands on the other shore calling Come Come Come."

"This town is full of soldiers and criminals and crazy people," my friend says. "It tires me out just to be here, but it's soothing, sitting on the porch with an intelligent woman like you. Are you staying long?"

"That depends," I say, sizing him up. It is fairly obvious that his left eye is made of glass. An armoured car goes by, disguised as a piece of jungle. It carries a gun as long as an elephant's trunk. He sighs.

"Yes Sir, lots of loonies around. Have you ever been to Smiths Falls?"

"Smiths Falls?" I say. "No, I don't believe I have."

"It's about twenty miles north of here," he says. "They put butter on your fries and on the hot dogs sold at stands. Great big hospital there and a home for the retarded. You should see them shopping in the Shopping Mall. You should see them eating hot dogs smeared with butter."

I'm tired out from the journey. I'm wrung out from all the heat and conversation. I go inside and get my key and go upstairs to sleep. I arrange to meet my friend for dinner.

But at dinner there's another message for me. It's disguised as a paper placemat, but I'm nobody's fool. It pretends to advertise a rock group coming to the hotel pub next door.

BOP TIL YOU DROP

it says,

BOP TIL YOU DROP

I excuse myself and go upstairs and start packing.

Relics

Relics

"Put your money in your left hand," the gypsy says. (THE ORIGINAL GYPSY ROSE LEE. PATRONIZED BY ALL CLASSES. SHE STANDS ALONE IN HER PRIVATE BUSINESS. ADVICE ON ALL MATTERS. STEP INSIDE.) She sits across from me at a table covered in grey satin. By her left elbow is an enormous cup of milky tea. I wonder if fortune tellers can see into their own futures and, if so, whether there is a high rate of suicide in this profession. But I do not ask; I am determined not to open my mouth. That way she will not immediately spot me for an American. ("You have made a journey across the water.")

Not for one minute do I believe that she is the original Gypsy Rose Lee; she's far too young. My ex-mother-in-law, in perhaps the only frivolous gesture of her entire adult life, consulted the original Gypsy Rose Lee in Blackpool in 1925. She told me the woman was "very handsome and in the prime of life." So unless this woman knows some way of appearing forever in her prime — and if she did, surely she'd be out marketing it instead of reading palms and tea leaves at second-rate country fairs? — she can not be the original.

> Gypsy Rose was very thin
> Gypsy Rose sat on a pin
> Gypsy…rose.

My name, too, is Rose and that's what the kids in the schoolyard used to yell at me. We knew about Gypsy Rose, or *a* Gypsy Rose, even in small towns in New York State in the late forties. I hated my name then; I wanted to be called Sally or Linda or Cathy. "Rose" was somehow not quite right. My mother, who had the perfectly respectable name of Helen, said that she had called me Rose because all the June roses were blooming in the garden when I was born. I asked why my sister had not been named Snowflake instead of Ruth.

But as I grew older I discovered the name had its compensations, lots of floral tributes from lovers and would-be lovers, for instance, when birthdays and anniversaries rolled around. Open any large book on my bookshelf and there's a fairly good chance that a pressed rose will fall out — mostly roses of a faded red, for I am not only tall and thin, I have very dark hair, a throwback to some dark Celt I suppose, since the rest of my family are ginger-haired and freckled. Red suits me, red dresses and red roses.

I have chosen a palm reading over tea leaves or crystal gazing, but to be honest I wouldn't be here if I really believed she could see into the future. I don't want to know. It's hard enough dealing with the past, and the events of this day have been almost too much for me, more than I can handle. What am I doing here? What do I hope she will say?

The gypsy scrutinizes my palm. Her fingernails are long and lacquered scarlet and, as she bends her head, I can see the grey along her part.

"You're a fool to yourself," she says without looking up. "You're a fool to yourself and a friend to many." She stares more intently into my palm.

"A married man is in love with you," she says.

I want to reply, "That's the story of my life. Some married man or other is always in love with me. I am that sort of woman." I want to show her the letter I am carrying around in my purse right now.

"Pull your panties down," he writes, "and put your hand between your legs and think of me." I am suddenly afraid and automatically try to pull away, but she shakes her head and smiles.

"You've never wanted to hurt anyone," she says. (Not true! Not true! I have been one of the world's careless people. I always make it a stipulation that I do not want to meet the wives, to see pictures of them or of the adorable children. Not for their sake but for mine.)

"You will write a play."

I ask no questions; I only smile and listen and nod.

When my time is up, I hand over my two pounds and go back down the steps of the caravan and out onto the street. Two elderly Scots women are standing near the bottom of the steps having a mild argument. One says to the other, "If it's no wurruth it, I'm no goin' in." They stare at me to see if I look like a satisfied customer and I smile my encouragement.

What shall I do now? It's not too early to go in search of a cup of tea. I'm staying the night so I don't have to think about buses or trains until tomorrow. Amazing how little this place has changed in twenty-five years. A launderette, a few more cafés, but essentially it's the same. Even MacArthurs Tea Room is still there, and the ridiculous sign — "For a Perfect Tea" with a picture of a golf club and ball. When I was a student here, we spent a lot of time in MacArthurs, eating scones and jam and drinking tea.

> Gaudeamus igitur,
> Iuvenes dum sumus.

"Let us rejoice then while we are young." We sang that at student gatherings and wore scarlet gowns to classes. It was all so romantic, and Americans love Romance. A ruined castle, a ruined cathedral, a commemorative plaque for the first student martyr, Patrick Hamilton. We were Americans: imagine a student martyr, imagine being burned to death for your beliefs! (The witches of Salem were somehow different, I suppose, because they were not students.)

Lammas Fair, this is, the ancient Feast of the First Loaf degenerated into a tawdry fun-fair running the length of New Street.

> World's Smallest Kilted Man
> He's Alive! 2'9" Tall, 29 Years Old

Rides called "The Ribtickler" and "The American Looper." A notice that no obscene photographs are to be exhibited.

> Taylor's Paratrooper
> (Pay Here)

Wilmot's Royal Televised Golden
Electric Carousel
Noted for Pleasing Young and
Old With Safety and Comfort

I'm almost tempted by that. We had a grand merry-go-
round in a park in my home town. When I was small,
my mother would sit with me in a sort of swan boat
while my sister, who was older as well as braver, would
go up and down beside us on a painted horse. Later I
rode the horses too. I had a favourite, black with a gold
bridle, and I was not above pushing and shoving to
make sure that was the horse I got. I would go back
again and again (the attendant made you get off and
stand in line until the whistle blew once more).
Sometimes I came away lurching like a drunk and once
I even threw up my lunch on the grass outside.

    The smell of chips and hot dogs, popcorn and candy
floss.

I have been back to the boarding house where I used to
live. It's a bed and breakfast place now, with a neat sign
out in front. Morag is dead. The new landlady told me,
wiping her hands on her white apron. Morag was dead
and her brother was in an asylum. "He was drrunk," she
said, rolling her *r*'s in disapproval. "She'd been leanin'
out the car window. Her head came off." The woman
lowered her voice to say this last, but it still sounded
shocking in the tidy street. So shocking I didn't really
take it in.

    "I was a student here once," I said. "A long time ago.
I wonder if it would be possible to see my old room?"

    "It might be occupied."

"The large room on the top floor, directly above the stairs."

She hesitated, and I could see she wanted to tell me it was occupied and that would mean telling a lie. But in the end she gave a curt nod and let me in.

The old dining-room to the left had been repapered and I could see through the door that it contained six or seven small tables covered with white cloths. A hand-written sign by the door announced that breakfast was from 7 to 9 A.M. inclusive, with "inclusive" underlined in red.

"Students," the landlady said and sniffed as she followed me up the stairs. This was a respectable place now; she wanted no truck with students. "The place was filthy," she said, "*filthy*," and stopped on the top step to look over her shoulder at me as though it were all somehow my fault.

"Well it's very nice now."

"A credit to you," I added, remembering a handy phrase my father-in-law had been fond of.

I stood at the door of my old room. It seemed smaller than I remembered it — such rooms usually do — and the gas fire was gone. Either she shut down in the winter months or had installed central heating. I couldn't believe the latter; there was something mean and frugal even in the way she got her words out of her mouth, as though she resented wasting her very breath. When we were students, we never had enough shillings for the gas fire and in any event it only really warmed a small area just in front of the fire. If we sat too close we got chilblains, in a waffle pattern, on our legs and they itched like crazy. We spent a lot of time studying or talking, while sitting in bed. When people came to visit, they kept their coats or gowns on or popped into bed with us. It was a bit like bundling. We wore woollen vests, even underneath our night-gowns, and stood around in the kitchen after supper, twelve of us, waiting for the big kettle to boil so we could fill our hot-water bottles. We moaned and bitched a lot but we didn't really care — or at least my room-mate and I, "the American girls," didn't care. This was *life*; this was the way students should live — penniless, eating rotten food, gathered under blankets and overcoats, boys and girls together, listening to "The Goon Show" on Tuesday nights, or hurrying along the streets on our way to lectures, the wind from the North Sea at our backs, our scarlet gowns like splashes of tropical flowers against the grey stone buildings of the Scottish town.

A fool to myself, am I, and a friend to many? Well, the first part may be true. But I was certainly no friend to Morag — none of us were. Oh, we talked to her from time to time but we never got involved with her, never asked her to come to the cinema to "watch how the Americans won the War," as some of our fellow boarders put it, never asked her to come up to our rooms for a drink or a chat. Only the French girl, Chloe, had anything like a friendship with her, and Chloe was not "one of us"; she did not go to University but to Teachers' Training College and got reduced rent for helping out in the kitchen. She was a large, plain girl with a dark moustache, old before her time and always in a bad mood, hating Scotland and at war, generally, with the whole world. We could hear her down in the kitchen (which was in the basement), complaining, airing her latest grievance, and could hear from time to time the sound of Morag's soft reply. Chloe thought we were fools; we thought she was boring.

I know that Morag had never been to university. She married young and had a baby; her husband existed only as a smiling photo in a silver frame. Chloe had seen it. She said he had been handsome and that there were no wedding photos. She must have volunteered this information because none of us were very curious about Morag, and I find that curious now. I think she was in awe of us and expected to be ignored. Her mother had died the previous summer and this was the first year Morag was running the place on her own. And we were used to someone else — our mothers, or in our case the cooks and maids at college back home — doing most of the domestic work. We more or less took it for granted, all of us, that we had to be left free for higher things. Men who lived in digs usually found a girlfriend to look after them.

Just before I came up to Scotland this time, I spent an afternoon in the British Museum, in the Duveen Gallery, looking at the Elgin Marbles. Why did I copy down in my notebook, while looking at the bits of frieze depicting the Battle of the Lapiths and Centaurs, "The head of the Centaur is in the Louvre, and that of the Lapith in Athens?" I suppose at the time I thought it strange and rather sad that these two figures, locked in a fight to the death on the walls of the British Museum, should have to stay there forever, headless, even though their heads in fact existed. I have always loved the Parthenon frieze. The guides say that this battle, won in the end by the Lapiths, represents the triumph of civilization over savagery. Maybe. The cen-taurs were unused to wine. They didn't know they were

supposed to water it down. It was too strong for them
and they got drunk and nasty. I like looking at the
muscles in the arms and legs of the Lapiths, in the
haunches of the centaurs. "The body dies; the body's
beauty lives."

Where is Morag buried? Who picked up her head?
Duncan, her brother? No wonder he went mad. Can a
head come off like that, be sliced right off? Surely not.
They went out of control and hit a road sign. Were they
having an argument or was he taking her out for a Sunday drive? Why was he drunk? He was a lawyer when I
was a student. Sometimes he would come to visit
Morag, I think to check on her. He had what Charles
Dickens would call a letter-box mouth, and I'm sure the
present landlady would have met with Duncan's
approval.

Somewhere a clock chimed the quarter hour and the
landlady cleared her throat.

"Is there anything else you're wanting?"

I shook my head. Then, "Do you still have the dumb-
waiter in the dining room? We used to ride up and
down in it, just for fun."

She frowned. "We got rid of it and installed a new
one." She had the front door open before I reached the
bottom of the stairs.

"Well," she said, managing a tight smile, "you've had
yur wee trip down Memory Lane, haven't ye?" She
seemed overly angry and sarcastic. I hadn't done anything to her.

"There was a daughter," I said, "She'd be about thirty-
five now."

"I'm sure I don't know," she said, and shut the door
in my face.

I walked down the steps and along the street, in the

direction of the ruined castle. I suppose every one of us has friends from our childhood or youth whom we have lost touch with and sometimes wonder about. But in some strange way we always assume that they are still there, right where we left them — perhaps we need them to be right there where we left them, as though they were pieces on a chess board. The game may have been interrupted but it would not be impossible to take it up again. Morag's death and the manner of her death acted like a terrible red scrawl on the nice pastel canvas of my day of nostalgia. I wished I hadn't come back. I wished I didn't know.

I stopped for a minute under the street-lamp. (I had a feeling the landlady was watching me from behind the dining-room curtains next door.)

I kissed my first lover under that street-lamp at 4 A.M. one winter morning, with the snow falling and his cum still sticky on the inside of my thighs. My second lover too — under that street-lamp and under many others, and in doorways, on the beach, by the castle, in one of the sand traps at the Royal and Ancient, in the back seat of his Morris Oxford which smelled of leather and Balkan Sobranie cigarettes. I couldn't get enough of it — the kissing, the touching. He was in the RAF and wore an overcoat of a lovely blue, almost a powder blue. Sometimes the sky looks like that, back home and I imagine it made of rough wool, I imagine my face pressed against it, and remember the way his coat smelled in the snow or the rain, remember his hands in my hair.

(Morag, did you ever cry from sheer exhaustion? Three flights of stairs to climb from the basement, dragging the old Hoover. And we were mean to you, sent food back down on the dumb-waiter if we didn't like it or even absented ourselves *en masse,* one night, without saying a word to you, when it was rissoles again for dinner. We pooled our money and ordered rounds of sandwiches and beer at the Cross Keys Hotel. Did you and your daughter have those rissoles night after night for supper until you couldn't stand the sight of them? Yet I don't remember you ever saying a mean word to any of us. We were like bratty children who have the upper hand and the parent knows it. We were "paying guests." How old were you then? Thirty? Thirty-two? Younger? I see you still in your old wool dressing-gown, standing in the hall of the dimly lit basement as I try to let myself in quietly, my mouth swollen and buzzing, my hair wild, my stockings in my handbag. "Rose, is that you?")

Come Landlord Fill the Flowing Bowl
Before The Night Grows Older

Come Landlord Fill the Flowing Bowl
Before the Night Grows Older

For Tonight We'll Merry Merry Be

For Tonight We'll Merry Merry Be

For Tonight We'll Merry Merry Be

Tomorrow We'll be Sober

"You lot always seem to be having such a good time." Several tables had been pushed together and I ended up sitting next to the flight lieutenant and his wife.

I nod. He is handsome in a George Sanders way, with a slightly nasal, slightly bored voice. He and his wife spend quite a lot of time in the Cross Keys; which is surprising as they live out of town, in Dunino, and there are nearer pubs as well as the Officers' Mess on the RAF base. I supposed they were bored and found the student crowd more jolly. We liked them because they were slightly exotic and because they bought us drinks. Later, when his wife had left him and run away with a student — one of our friends in fact, although not a member of the boarding house — I realized she may have been looking for someone all along. Her name was Ursula and she didn't say much, just sat there with an amused, slightly contemptuous look on her face. She was blonde, very thin, very attractive, and wore gold-rimmed glasses long before they were in style. When she did speak she had a marvellous husky voice, but most of the time she just sat there. Sometimes she even read a book. It was said that she had had a bad time as a young girl in Germany during the War. All the boys were in love with her. They lit her cigarettes and tossed coins to see who would sit next to her, and she just laughed at them or said "sank you" in her Marlene Dietrich voice. I didn't pay too much attention to either of them for I was in love and was very busy daydreaming about life as a missionary's wife on the Gold Coast or some such place. The object of my affection was a dark-haired, kilted theology student from Inverness. Needless to say, I attended Chapel every day and had joined the Afro-Asian Society, where I danced with young men who still startle me, sometimes, when their faces appear, older and plumper, in newspaper photos of political leaders of certain countries. And I was very busy generally. The courses I was taking required a lot of reading and essay-writing. The papers came back marked with Greek letters, Alpha, Beta, Gamma, α, β, γ, and usually with the comment: "Your handwriting is execrable." I was determined to do well, although the methods of instruction were confusing to someone like myself, more used to being told that an assignment was due next Wednesday than to hearing a professor read out a list of books "which might be of interest" and then discovering questions about these books on the first exam. Alpha, Beta, Gamma, Delta…how strange, how much more musical than A, B, C, D, E. Latin songs, Greek marks, castles, cathedrals, references to John Knox and Mary Queen of Scots — we lapped it all up and wrote silly pretentious letters to our friends and family back home. I suppose we imagined ourselves to be living a life that was somehow more "real" than anything we could be offered in the States and perhaps we were; but not in terms of those letters — my mother saved them and later passed them on to me. They are full of new words, "Senior Man," "Senior Woman," "bejantine," "gaudy," "Raisin Monday." We took snapshots of each other, in our scarlet gowns and mortar-boards walking along the pier after chapel on Sunday, or leaning against a piece of the ruined cathedral wall. How young I look. How serious. I look at those photos and think, "Now there's a girl who will go places."

The British girls did not shave their legs or their armpits. Several girls we knew went to bed with their boyfriends. One or two even lived with their young men. I would see them out walking or at the cinema or having tea at MacArthurs and wonder what it was like, to wake up in the morning next to a man, to let him see you tangle-haired and grumpy, perhaps with your breath not sweet or your period started. Sometimes I would blush just looking at these couples, just imagining all the little intimacies of their daily lives together.

It seemed very brave somehow, to allow oneself to be exposed like that.

And then one night at the Cross Keys I had an accident. I was wearing my favourite skirt, of pale beige wool and cashmere, and I also had my period. When I realized what was happening I was afraid it was already too late and there would be blood, not only on the back of my skirt but on the seat as well. The lieutenant's greatcoat was slung casually over the back of his chair and he was standing at the bar, talking. I leaned over and whispered to Ursula: "Do you think he'd mind if I borrowed his coat for a minute; I have to go to the Ladies." I was blushing with embarrassment, and afraid she might laugh at me. But she figured it all out very quickly, reached over and took the coat off the chair; as I stood up she threw it over my shoulders.

In the Ladies it was just as I had feared — a great reddish stain all over the back of my pale skirt. I had only a heavy cardigan with me, not a coat and how was I to get a message to someone at the table to run home (it wasn't very far) and get me something, anything, to wrap around me? I resigned myself to waiting until somebody I knew came in to pee or until somebody missed me and came to see if I was all right.

(What if there were blood all over the seat? What if everyone knew?)

Then Ursula came in and I told her, I showed her what had happened. She nodded. "I'll ask Nicky to drive you home. Just keep the coat over your shoulders and come out with me now." The fact that her husband would now know what happened embarrassed me even more, but I was so grateful to her that I followed her out meek as a lamb. She went up to the bar and whispered to him and he turned to me and smiled.

"That coat becomes you," he said. "Shall we go?"

I nodded, too miserable to speak. Ursula said she was going back to the table and he could pick her up after he delivered me safely home.

A strange beginning to a love affair. I sat hunched and miserable in one corner of the car, not saying anything except my address, praying the blood wouldn't go through to his beautiful coat as well. He parked the car and said, "I'll walk you to the house, shall I, and see you safely inside?" I nodded and he came round to open my door. As I stepped out onto the curb I fainted, "dropped like a shot bird" as Nick said later.

Morag, what did you think when an RAF officer arrived on your doorstep with an unconscious girl in his arms? I never asked and you never said. I was too humiliated, then, to ask questions. I woke up in bed, the sharp smell of ammonia in my nostrils and you sitting beside me with a worried expression on your face. The doctor came a few minutes later and prescribed some pills. They came in a small round red box with a label pasted to the top. "For female complaints" it said, and my name. Nicky had left, you said, right after he had called the doctor.

Morag, your husband was a Polish officer. Your married name was long and full of consonants — it began with *W* and ended in -ski. Was he dead or were you divorced before "the American girls" came to the boarding house? What did you think of me and my affair with Nicky? You seemed about to say something once but I brushed past you and ran lightly up the stairs.

"Rose, is that you?" knowing perfectly well it was, standing there in the doorway of your dark bedroom, "Rose, I..."

"It's late," I said, fleeing, "I'll see you in the morning."

What did a flight lieutenant do? ("left-tenant left-tenant," naked inside his greatcoat I would tease him, "left-tenant," "*left*-tenant, how funny.") He never told me very much. He was probably a "gentleman officer" (Sandhurst etc.) for he lived off the base and seemed to have money of his own. He was certainly a career officer and if he'd joined the Air Force when he was eighteen he must have been near retirement even then. "I am the equivalent of your Captain," he said, but since that meant nothing to me I made a joke of it.

> You are the Captain of my fate;
> you are the Captain of my soul.

He told me he was a pilot and he wore wings over his left pocket to prove it; but where he flew to, or why, was never mentioned. Perhaps he simply flew to keep up his skills. Once he said that being in the RAF in peacetime was "mind-numbing," was "boring." "It's mostly booze and darts."

I liked it that we had to sneak around at night, for I was awkward and shy in my long bones and I had no breasts to speak of. I had my first orgasm standing up against a part of the castle wall. I did not know about orgasms, that women "came" and it had certainly never happened with my first lover (who had lasted a mere two weeks). I didn't know what had happened. When I was three years old I took one of my mother's long hairpins and stuck it in an electrical outlet. I can still remember my whole arm buzzing, as though I had been stung. And crying out, being comforted, barely able to stand, my body ticking over like a cooling car. It was chilly and there was a mist and I kept my face pressed into the damp wool of his coat. "Oh my God," I said, "oh my God."

Lammas Fair. To do with the gathering of the first corn. Long ago men in the fields ejaculated onto the ground or couples fucked to ensure a good crop.

He never mentioned "Taking precautions," nor did I. Do couples still use that phrase, "Taking precautions"? It's a wonder I didn't get pregnant. What would I have done. There was one American girl we knew who had got married the year before to her Scots boyfriend. Had to get married. He was away somewhere but she occasionally came to parties. Once she even brought her baby and nursed him, sitting in an armchair and chatting to some fellow who stood over her. I was shocked.

Morag, I have come to the cemetery to see if I can find your grave. Did they put your head back on your body before they buried you? Was that woman lying? Did your daughter stand alone and mourn? If I'd known, I would have sent something — roses. I want to find you, but it's getting chilly; I need my tea.

"In Memory of Miss Fairlee of Colinton"
"Miss Magdalene Scott"
"Jean Fairfoul"

and James Webster, the unfortunate fifth son of the Rev. James Webster of Inverarty, Forfarshire

a distinguished student
at St. Andrews University
Destined for the English bar
He entered the Inner Temple
But while travelling in the East

His career was
Prematurely Closed
Anxious to see the spot
Where the Divine Law was Proclaimed
He made the Ascent of Mount Sinai
But on his return to Cairo
He was seized with fever
which terminated fatally
on 1st August 1829
In his Twenty-Seventh Year

"Little Alec — born in Calcutta — 1895-1899
Thy Will Be Done"

A woman named Jennet

A woman named Jessie

Mrs Mary Overton

Relict of Harry Hope

The French destroyed the castle because the Protestants
murdered Beaton. We put on *Macbeth* here in the spring.
I was one of the witches, with silvered hair and a pale
green face. Nicky and Ursula came to see me perform.
("Behold, where stands the usurper's cursed head.")
There was a cast party afterwards and I got quite drunk.
At about one in the morning I left, make-up removed
but still with my silver hair, and walked down to the sea.
What was going to become of me? I had reached the
point where the sight of Nicky's fingers gently drumming on a table at the Cross Keys sent such waves of excitement through me, such electricity, that I would have
to get up and leave. He felt it too, or said he did
when I told him; but he may have, most probably

had, felt it before, maybe even with Ursula, although I never saw them touch.

Once, when I was walking down the street with my husband, shortly after our first child was born, walking arm in arm in the late spring sunshine, the baby at home with her grandparents for an hour, I thought of the child and how beautiful she was and how much I loved her and my breasts filled up with milk, became so heavy and hungry for her mouth, they overflowed and leaked milk all over the front of my pale blue dress. I borrowed my husband's cardigan and hurried home. And then such relief, such pleasure. When I looked at Nicky's fingers drumming on the table, his index finger and middle finger which had explored me so thoroughly and satisfactorily I felt something not unlike what I felt later, walking arm in arm with my husband and thinking of my child. A different kind of love, of course, that of a woman for a man or a woman for her child but the visceral intensity was the same. What was to become of me, to become of us both? It was June. As soon as term ended, my room-mate and I were going on a walking tour of the Highlands. She knew about Nicky, of course (and disapproved), and she was in love with a young medical student. But we had promised ourselves this tour and even love wasn't going to get in the way. Or so she said and I felt I had to go along with it or she'd never forgive me. Right after the trip she was leaving to spend some time with relatives in England, then sailing home. I would come back here for two weeks and then I too was leaving for the States.

But when we came back, Ursula had run away to London and Nicky was all alone.

Morag, I can't find your grave; I can't even kneel

down and call to you through your blanket of grass and earth and wood. "Forgive me. Forgive me." I think you were terribly lonely, trying to run that house all by yourself after your mother died, trying to raise your pretty, sulky daughter. If I had known then all of the things that I know now.

("Is that you Rose? Would you like to stop and have a cup of tea?")

It is cold today and the sea looks cold, indigo col-oured. I hope there is an electric heater in the room recommended to me by the pretty girl in the Tourist In-formation Office. I forgot to look. I just dumped my things and signed the register and ran out. Why did I come back here? Like Thomas in the Bible, do I have to touch the wound before I will believe? But whose wound? Mine? Hers? His? Down in the sand there are children with spades and buckets and I can hear the sound of the sea: a steady, sandy sound and yet at the same time the sound of wind in a forest. The train doesn't come all the way here anymore. You have to take a bus from Leuchars Junction.

I moved in with him. He had packed up all of Ur-sula's stuff in boxes but had not yet sent it on. I slept with him in their bed; I went with him to the Officers' Mess; I was open and arrogant and unafraid. Nothing was real and yet everything had the intensity of a fever or a dream. I did not cook or clean. During the day, while he was at the base, I slept. Around four o'clock I took a bath and dressed. Then he came home and bathed and we went out. He had one very curious habit; he always slept with his socks on. I knew there was nothing wrong with his feet for I had seen him in the bath. But he always slept in his socks. Perhaps he had cold feet; I never asked.

When it was time for me to leave he drove me to

Edinburgh and from there I was to take the train to London and then to Southampton. We had tea at the North British Hotel. It was only in the last hour that I began to cry. He asked me to come back and marry him when I had finished my degree and he was free. I hadn't expected that. I said "yes" and he kissed me through my tears but we both knew I didn't mean it. I suppose I was so young that I knew I had my whole life before me. Now — what would I do in such a situation now?

When I went to pack up all my things and say goodbye to Morag (the rest of the house, Chloe and the other students, had already "gone down" as they call it here) she asked if I had time to stop and have a cup of tea. She was in the great gloomy kitchen with its huge black Aga cooker, peeling potatoes for her supper.

"I'm sorry," I said. "I'll be sure to write."

"Rose, I…" And then she turned back to the potatoes and that was all.

Now I lie in a soft bed underneath the eaves and I cannot sleep. I walked back through the town before supper. Jets from the airbase suddenly screamed over my head. I walked under the arch and into the quadrangle of St Salvator's College, "my" college. It was very peaceful and quiet in there. On the bulletin board, amidst items WANTED or FOR SALE

(FREE, TO A GOOD HOME
A HORSE
-hair mattress/

was a notice about a crisis line, dial 5555. In white balloons on a blue background typical crises were written:

"Somehow University isn't quite what I expected"

"I think I might be homosexual"

"I've missed two periods"

"I've just taken an overdose"

There were second-hand Anglo-Saxon texts for sale:

The Battle of Maldon

The Dream of the Road

The Wanderer

The Seafarer

("I can/about myself/a song/utter.")

Nicky, where are you now, I thought. He would no longer be an "older man," just an aging one. "Let us rejoice while we are young." Everything seemed numinous. The play at the new Byre Theatre was *A Profusion of Red Roses*.

I saw a teenage girl, perhaps Gypsy Rose's daughter, staring out the back window of her caravan as I walked by. Does her mother tell *her* fortune?

And now I lie in bed and a clock strikes in the town. Ten ... Eleven ... Twelve.

"We have heard the chimes at midnight, Master Shallow."

Shortly after I returned to college, one of the younger girls in our house came up to borrow a dress. Nicky's picture was on my bureau, quite a large picture, 8x10, that he had sent me. It had been taken as a publicity photo for some play he was in a few years earlier and I had admired it.

I didn't know this girl very well. She stood, the dress over her arm, and looked around my room. She saw the photo in its place of honour.

"Is that your father?" she said. "Gosh, he's handsome." He was too young to be my father. Why didn't I contradict her?

After she had gone downstairs, I took the photo and put it in a drawer. I never wrote to him again or answered his telegrams or accepted any of his phone calls.

Goodbye Harold,
Good Luck

Goodbye Harold,
Good Luck

She had felt safe, or at least safely defined, so long as her daughter was with her; a mother travelling with a child was not an unusual sight. But now in the lounge of the Inn, her daughter watching Elvis Presley in *Jailhouse Rock* upstairs in their room, with the door locked and bolted and an agreed-upon signal of knocks set up before she would let anyone, even her mother, inside, Francine was exposed for what she really was — a woman alone in a bar.

She found herself pushing her hair back all the time, so that the waitress, at least, would see that she wore a wedding ring. Then it might be assumed that she was waiting for her husband, a man who sold tractors or farm equipment, or an engineer who'd gone on a tour of the dam. Or perhaps the wedding ring was false. It was, in a way, wasn't it; for to the wearer, at least, it was not the symbol it was to the rest of the world. Lately the wearer saw it as a small gold tourniquet tied too tight, cutting off her circulation, not just to that finger but all over. Francine had been having trouble breathing and had begun yoga classes hoping they would help her relax. Twice a week, she and seven other women lay on a carpeted floor in the neighbourhood community centre and practised breathing or tensed and relaxed their thighs and buttocks against the carpeting. The instructor was a handsome, middle-aged East Indian doctor, Dr Bannerman, who always wore a beautiful sari and did not do any of the exercises or positions herself. "Shake it up, shake it up, shake it up, bounce bounce!" called Dr Bannerman in her sing-song voice. "Let go of it now, let go!" But Francine could not let go or at least could never quiet her mind, however much she tried to concentrate on a small blue lake between her eyebrows, a lake without a ripple, but deep, deep, deep and not a human being in sight, not a sound, not even the small "pock" of a fish jumping up to a fly. The breathing problem continued and was getting worse, not better. The other day she remembered a story she had read as a girl, Conan Doyle's "The Speckled Band." That's how it felt, as though something mysterious were strangling her and cutting off her air.

Perhaps it was simply the beginning of an old-fashioned nervous breakdown. Seeing one's wedding ring as a poisonous snake was pretty bizarre, was it not? And who would play Sherlock Holmes to her Helen? Who would come immediately and set everything to rights and send the snake back up the bell-pull before it struck; send it back up to strike the striker. She remembered that story so clearly. It was fun to be scared then. Francine remembered the bed in the story had been bolted to the floor.

She went to the doctor, who examined her

thoroughly and declared that he could find nothing wrong; he suggested she might like to be referred to a psychiatrist. Their family doctor had just retired and this was a young man, dark-haired and quite good-looking, who had taken over the practice. In the waiting-room the goldfish tank, which had always been covered in scum, so that the fish within were just dull orange smears, had been removed, and the walls were decorated with large matted photographs of Greece. When Francine admired them, the doctor said his wife had taken them last year on holiday. Francine wondered what his wife was like; lately she thought about wives a lot — other wives of other men. Did any of them walk around in a similar state of choking despair?

"I couldn't do that — go to a psychiatrist — unless my husband went as well and he never would. He'll say that I can go if it will make me feel any better, but that there's nothing wrong with him. He comes from a family where to say 'it's all in your head' implies that whatever is wrong is your own fault and you can correct it; you can shake it out of your head the way you would shake a pebble or a piece of grit out of your shoe."

The doctor looked at her and smiled.

"Do you think there is something wrong with him?"

"I think so. At any rate, he hates me." There it was, out in the open. He hated her and was trying to kill her or trying to kill her spirit. He was the deadly snake.

"Hate is a very strong word," the doctor said, "especially to use about the relationship between a husband and wife."

"He's a very strong man," she said.

The bus from Prince George had broadcast country

and western music for 170 miles. Francine liked that kind of music, even if it was sentimental; it dealt with the sad realities of people cheating on one another, hurting each other, lonely people in bars. A woman spelling out Dee-Eye-Vee-O-R-See-Eee so the little child listening won't know what she is talking about. But her daughter Emily was ten, not two or three; she knew how to spell.

The doctor suggested once again that she should talk to a psychiatrist. He offered to call her husband and talk to him. Francine shook her head.

"When I was young I used to take violin lessons," she said, "at a music store downtown. One week they re- placed the old door to the building with a fancy one made of glass. I didn't realize it was there and walked right into it. It gave me an awful shock as well as a bump on the head. Trying to talk to my husband is like that. You can't get through to him at all, although he *appears* to be open and inviting. Don't get me wrong — the bump on the head is just a metaphor — he doesn't lay a hand on me. But there are ways of hurting people..." She shook her head. "Do I sound melo- dramatic?"

The young doctor looked at her for several seconds, then shook his head.

"You sound discouraged."

"I am. And yet I love him. Or I did. Now I just don't know. He makes me feel such a failure and it isn't just me, it's our daughter as well. It's beginning to bother her."

"In what way?"

"Here's an example. Our daughter is left-handed and this is a right-handed world. She knocks things over sometimes. When my husband sets the table, and he often does, he sets it as though we were all right-handed. I think he does it on purpose. I try to remember to switch her glass, but sometimes I forget. She knocks her glass over — she does this in restaurants too — and he says, in his soft voice, 'My beautiful clumsy daughter, my beautiful clumsy daughter.'" (Francine didn't tell the doctor that he sometimes added, "her mother's child.")

"He makes me feel stupid, straightens things, turns the gas down lower when I'm cooking. He makes us both feel stupid. He says he's a perfectionist, but I think there's a fine line between a perfectionist and a bully."

"What does he do for a living?"

"He's a civil engineer. His specialty is concrete docks. I suppose one has to be a perfectionist when designing things like that; but human beings, well, human beings are programmed to be fallible. And the awful thing is that the more he expects us to be perfect, the more we break things or burn saucepans or generally disappoint him."

"Look here," the doctor said, "I think you need a psychiatrist *and* a marriage counsellor. And soon. I can give you some names."

"Thank you," Francine said, knowing she wouldn't use them. There was no point in her going alone. She put the list in her pocket.

Instead, she joined the yoga class and decided to take Emily on a trip, just the two of them, during Spring Break. Maybe, if she got right away, she'd be able to decide what to do.

Last week Francine had broken a wine glass. Two days later her husband had put down the newspaper and had looked at her smiling.

"What are we going to do about all this breaking of things?"

There was an entertainer in the middle of the lounge, a small woman, in her sixties maybe, with curly white permed hair. She had a sharp little face and a high quick voice and reminded Francine of a toy poodle. She would play a few bars on the piano, take a good swig of her drink and then tell a joke, a really filthy joke. Francine realized she'd been hearing this woman all along, without really listening, sitting alone at her table against the wall, sipping her beer, nervously pushing her hair back from her forehead, with her left hand. Now that she was paying attention, she was shocked. This woman was on the edge of being elderly; in spite of the heavy make-up, you could see the rumpled skin beneath. What was she doing in this place, dressed up like a toy poodle with a pink ribbon in her hair, yapping away, yap yap in her small high voice.

"And I says to him," yelled the poodle-woman, "keep your goddamn meatballs outta my spaghetti." She wheezed and coughed, laughing at her own joke.

Where had this woman come from, for God's sake; where was she going? Now Francine remembered a sandwich board outside the lounge as she came in. "Back by popular demand."

Could that be so? She'd been here before and had told jokes like this and people had wanted her back? The woman had a dog's name, as well, or the kind of name you'd give a poodle in a comic strip — Fifi, or Mimi or ZaZa.

They had subscribed to *The New York Review of Books* for

years and it had always been a joke between them to read out bits from the "Personals":

> "Oriental woman, who knows how to make a man happy, would like to meet kind millionaire who will marry and take care of her."

> "Retired gentleman, 65, unusually youthful in body."

> "DWF, attractive strawberry blonde (Clairol), 43 (really), seeks loving man for summer (or lifetime) romance."

When they first started reading the ads, Francine had said, "What's a DWF?" and her husband very quickly replied "Dwarf, it means dwarf." That became a joke between them too — that there were so many lonely dwarfs in New York City.

The poodle-woman struck a chord on the piano.

"But doctor," I said, "that's not my rectum!" Yap Yap.

"And this is no thermometer."

Few people were paying attention to the poodle-woman, "back by popular demand," although a group of men, quite drunk, were daring each other to pour a glass of beer over her head.

Francine made wet rings with the bottom of her glass. Would she be one of those dwarfs seeking "friendship and new beginnings" in the back pages of *The New York Review of Books*? "DWF with lovely ten-year-old daughter seeks...." Seeks what? She looked around at the men in the lounge. Seeks whom? "Seeks someone who is gentle and sometimes wrong."

A few weeks ago Francine had heard part of a program featuring a children's theatre group who were working in elementary schools — or a few selected elementary schools — to try to teach children not to go with strangers. They presented the play one way, where the child went off with a stranger who had convinced her to help him look for his lost puppy; and then they stopped and held a question-and-answer period with the kids. What could the little girl have done instead of agreeing to get in the stranger's car? What would *you* do? Francine had found the play or playlet — it was just a few minutes long — really frightening, but the children didn't seem frightened, perhaps because the players were right there talking to them afterwards. Then the play was performed again, and this time the "little girl" did all the safe, correct things. It was an interesting experiment, although some of the parents were now objecting. Francine started talking about it at the dinner table.

Emily listened quietly, then said: "I really can't understand anyone wanting to hurt a little kid. They must be sick."

"They are sick," Francine said. "That's the terrible thing. They're sick and then they get scared and then they're dangerous."

"I find it so hard to understand," Emily said.

"The whole world's sick," her father said. Francine looked at her husband, who had been quietly eating his dinner with a little smile on his face.

"It's just as sick to drive those idiotic noisy cars or eat at McDonald's," he said. "The whole world's sick."

Emily looked at him. "I don't think what we're talking about is the same thing as eating at McDonald's." She stood up. "Excuse me, I have homework to do."

"Why do you do that?" Francine asked when Emily had gone upstairs.

"Do what?" He was the picture of innocence, patting his lips with a napkin.

"Globalize everything; make statements like that. It makes kids — anyone — feel so helpless."

"I don't want her growing up to think the world is simple; it isn't. It's more than a question of strangers in cars."

"But what we were talking about was exactly that — strangers in parks, in cars. Emily was trying to understand how people could do these things, hurt a child."

"And I told her."

"You did *not!* You made a smart, sweeping statement and she left the table more confused than ever."

He then stood up, and mocking her, mocking all of it, dismissed himself.

"Excuse me, I have some homework of my own to do."

Francine ran her finger around the wet rings on the table.

So far, Emily had seen the trip as an adventure. They had taken the train from North Vancouver to Prince George, Emily reading out information from the brochure they'd been given with their tickets.

"'Mile 139.3. Seaton Portage. Site of the first railway in B.C.'

"'Mile 142.3. Shalalth. Gateway to famous Bridge River gold mining district.' Gold mines, Mom! Imagine that!

"'Horse Lake. Highest point on railway.' We're *three thousand, eight hundred and sixty-four feet* above sea level!"

She said it slowly, for emphasis.

The compartment wasn't full, even though the schools were on holiday. Most people couldn't afford the time, perhaps, unless they were tourists. There was a couple from Fiji with a little girl of about two. The baby ran down the aisle with a waddling run and was caught up by its father again and again. Emily made friends with the baby and soon she too was chasing it down the aisle, laughing. It was fun being on a train, looking at the world outside the window unrolling like a painted carpet.

An overweight woman with a little boy was talking to an older woman in the seat just behind.

"I don't care if it's her father or her uncle. If any man lays a hand on her, I want to know about it."

"Big tits!" shouted Fifi.

The room was filling up, and with more people coming in all the time, Francine realized she was the only woman sitting alone. There were a few couples and one table of women quite near the carpeted dais that served as a stage. The women all wore identical magenta sateen jackets with gold lettering on the back. "Queen Pins" the jackets said in fancy script: underneath was an anthropomorphic ten pin with long embroidered eyelashes and a pouty mouth, her hands on her "hips." The women were having a good time, talking and laughing and drinking beer. They paid no attention to the poodle-woman who, with a final chord and to very little applause, closed the piano and walked off.

"Stupid cunt," said one of the drunken men at the next table.

The women on the bowling team had elaborate hair-dos, almost like beehives, which must have taken a long time to arrange. None of them was really young. Perhaps they simply kept the same hairdos they had worn in high school or as young wives, the hairdos in their wedding photographs. Francine's hair had been long when she'd married, and she had kept it long, often braided in a single braid — for it was very thick and would not stay pinned up — until Emily was born. The baby had had a fierce grip and was always pulling her mother's hair. Francine didn't mind, but it hurt, it hurt a lot, and finally she had cut it short. It had been short ever since.

"DWF, thick brown hair, unable to breathe in former relationship seeks…" Seeks what?

Emily loved having lunch in their seats on the train and staying overnight at a motel in Prince George. Everything delighted and amused her: the drinking glasses, "sanitized for your protection," the paper seal on the toilet, the colour TV right in the bedroom. She immediately took a bath so she could use the miniature cake of soap and a packet of shampoo. The next morning she read the breakfast menu out loud: "*freshly* squeezed orange juice," "*farm fresh* eggs."

He wasn't a bad man, or not at first, and maybe not even now. He was very precise and loved order. Francine was untidy, forgetful, a compulsive saver of paper bags, string, leftovers. Every so often her husband would open the fridge and begin to pull things out. Six or seven cottage cheese containers full, or partly full, of leftovers. Wrinkled green peppers and bits of lettuce that looked like slimy seaweed. He often examined the fridge when she was out, sometimes making a collage of all the mess right in the middle of the kitchen table. Once he spelled her name in leftover fettucine. She laughed and promised to reform; but of course she never did.

"I hate waste," her husband said, "I just hate it."

Last autumn, when she was topping and tailing some carrots for dinner, he came up behind her and said, with quiet exasperation, "Francine, do you know how long it takes to grow a carrot?"

Of course she did! The carrots were from their own garden. She was so angry she threw down the paring knife and went for a long walk down to the sea. She stood looking out at the freighters and sailing boats, wishing he didn't have the power to upset her, wishing he weren't so often right. (For she had been cutting off the tops and bottoms any old which way, listening to a concert on the radio. To use his words, she had not been *paying attention*.) When she got back home, Emily was there alone, worried.

"Daddy went looking for you. Did you two have a fight?"

That night he apologized.

"You're impossible," she said. "You're too hard on people."

"I know. I can't help it. I'm just as hard on myself. I guess I'm just a dyed-in-the-wool perfectionist."

Then they made love.

She shouldn't have ordered beer because now she had to pee. She'd seen people getting up and going along a corridor to the left of the stage, so that's where the toilets were. She'd have to walk past a lot of tables to get there, the woman who had been sitting alone at the table by the wall, nursing a glass of beer. Of course she could go back up to the room. But she wanted to think, without Emily around, for just a little longer. She wanted to try and figure out what was the best thing to do.

The Mens said "STEERS" and the Ladies

"HEIFERS." As she was returning to her table, the lights grew dim. Then a red spot went on and a young blonde woman, wearing a red satin kimono with a dragon on the back, walked up onto the stage. Recorded music began — something with a heavy pounding beat, something Francine recognized but couldn't put a name to. The girl tossed her kimono into a corner. Now she was naked except for her red high heels. Didn't strippers strip? She licked her lips and began to dance. The room grew quiet.

"I do not want to watch this," Francine thought. "I must go now, before she gets right into it, before it would look odd to get up and leave." But she sat there, unable to move, curious. She had never seen a stripper before.

"Wait till she gets to the oil," said one of the men at the next table. "That's the best part. We're not gonna get stiff watching this."

"Speak for yourself," said another man, and they laughed.

"No. The towelling off's terrific. I saw her at lunchtime. She don't dance very good but she's got a nice body, no scars or stretchmarks or tatoos or nothing."

The girl had shaved off all her body hair. She played with her nipples as she danced, or pranced really. The man at the next table was right about her dancing. She licked her lips and put her tongue between her teeth, but she never smiled. How many shows had she done already today? Where had she come from? Where would she move on to? The girl looked tired. Once, when she bent over and put her head between her legs, Francine remembered Emily doing that, aged about three, looking at the world upside down between the arches of her chubby legs. Last week Emily had set the table as though they were all left-handed. Her father didn't notice and knocked over his wine glass. Emily gave a nasty little laugh. "Now you know what it feels like," she said.

Francine had seen a button in a women's bookstore.

THEY SENT ONE MAN TO THE MOON WHY CAN'T THEY SEND THEM ALL?

It was funny, but not really. Would Emily grow up hating men? The woman on the train was worried about some adult putting his arm around her daughter; what happened if the opposite were true, never a hug or kiss?

Daaa/dah dah dah dah dah dah dah/dah dah daaa. It was "Bolero," of course, the music the girl was dancing to. She stopped a minute to spread a heavy piece of plastic on the stage. There, with the start of a new riff, something slow and sensuous, she squirted oil all over herself and lay down, the plastic bottle in her right hand, her legs in the air, moving to the music. She put her hand between her legs.

"You know why they have that red light on them," said one of the men at the next table. "Makes their flesh look good. They won't dance without it."

"Listen to the expert," said his companion.

"Shut up," said the third man, "I'm trying to concentrate."

"Keep your hands on the table, Vern," said the first man, laughing.

"Seeking..."? "Seeking a friendly surveyor." How about that? Someone to lay out her life for her, establish boundaries and elevations, like George Dawson, who laid out this district. But perhaps that would be too much like an engineer? Except that surveyors had to take into account natural curves and irregularities. Later on the engineers moved in and straightened things out. Just before sunset, she and Emily had walked over to the Mile 0 post to take each other's pictures.

"One thousand, five hundred and twenty-three miles to Fairbanks," Emily said. "Maybe we can go there sometime."

"Would you like that?"

"Sure. Can we have room service when we go back to the motel? And can I ring down and order?"

"Yes. Spoiled brat."

"Am I?"

"No, you're not." She didn't tell Emily that they had come to Dawson Creek because of Mile 0, because Francine had heard about it once from her husband and had liked the sound of it — "Mile 0." And they could take a train and then a bus, see something of the province. (And possibly just keep going, that thought was there too. And possibly just keep going. If I think about him as "he," Francine decided. If I think about him only as "he" it will be easier. He did, he did not.)

The pretty blonde girl was finishing her act, writhing on the slippery sheet, running her hands over her body, her face as expressionless as when she'd begun. The music stopped and she stood up, walked over to a chair and began to towel herself off. Her face changed; she looked relaxed and almost happy and began to chat with some men at a nearby table. The man at the next table to Francine, the man who had seen the lunch-time show, called out "Donna! Hey honey, c'mover

here and I'll buy you a drink." She smiled in his direction, nodded and continued towelling herself off. She
looked like a girl who had just come out of a pool after
a good swim. Except for her curious hairlessness of
course; presumably that was so the men could see her
touch herself. Francine wondered if all strippers shaved
themselves. The only time she'd ever been shaved was
when Emily was born and she hadn't liked it. As the
hair grew back in, it was very prickly and it itched. Her
husband said it felt like a wheat field in autumn. He
was a good man, a good lover. But something was terribly wrong.

The girl walked over to the table where the three
men were sitting. She nodded at Francine and gave her
a cheerful smile. There was a pervasive, familiar smell
now coming from that table. What was it? Something
Francine knew, knew well.

Johnson's Baby Oil. The girl had been rubbing
herself, squirting herself, with Johnson's Baby Oil! How
funny! Most of these men would be married; most
would have kids. Perhaps the Johnson's Baby Oil
worked as some kind of subliminal turn-off and the girl
was aware of that, it was her private joke. Francine had
used Johnson's Baby Oil as suntan oil when she was a
teenager. All her friends did; it was cheaper than suntan lotion. But they washed it off before they went out
with their boyfriends; they wouldn't have been caught
dead using it any place but on the beach.

Francine got up and left the lounge. It was almost
time for the place to close.

After supper, which they ate on a table in front of the
television, Emily had said she wanted to take a shower
and wash her hair. (More small soaps, more sachets of
shampoo.)

"All right," Francine said, "but hurry. You'll have to get your hair dry before you go to sleep. That's an order."

Emily went into the bathroom and shut the door. Francine heard the water running and then it stopped.

"Mom," Emily called through the door. "Come here." Her voice sounded strange, excited.

Francine went into the bathroom. Emily stood there naked, a pink towel wrapped around her head, staring at the mirror. The steam from the shower had brought out a message.

'Goodbye Harold, Good Luck.' Written by somebody's finger or with a piece of soap. Goodbye Harold, Good Luck. Even the comma was there.

They laughed and laughed.

"Who do you suppose did it?" Emily said.

"I don't know I'm sure."

Francine wondered what sort of a motel they were in, but it had been recommended by their travel agent. She wondered about the beds. Would there be enormous stains on the mattresses, underneath the sheets? That's when she decided on the knocks, the password, before she would leave her daughter alone.

Who wrote it? Somebody who got up and left while Harold was still sleeping. Somebody who knew him — or men — well enough to know he'd take a shower in the morning. But maybe he hadn't. Surely anyone who had been left a message like that would want to rub it out?

Was it Donna, the stripper, the girl in the red kimono? Was it written with an oily finger?

Francine knocked three times, gave the password and said, "It's Mum." Emily, half-asleep, let her in.

That would be one way to do it of course. Pack her

bags, and Emily's, and leave forever one day when her husband, when *he*, was on a trip. Write her farewells on the mirror, perhaps with a piece of soap saved especially from the Inn. He'd come home, take a shower, step out and see it. Goodbye, goodbye. Good luck. Could she do it? The idea was certainly attractive.

"Mum," Emily said from the other bed, "were you ever in love with Elvis Presley when you were a girl?"